On a Clear April Morning

A Jewish Journey

Jewish Latin American Studies

Series Editor: Darrell B. Lockhart (University of Nevada, Reno)

MARCOS IOLOVITCH

On a Clear
April Morning

A Jewish Journey

Translated by
MERRIE BLOCKER

BOSTON
2020

This novel is published with support from the Brazilian National Library Foundation (Fundação Biblioteca Nacional).

Obra publicada com o apoio da Fundação Biblioteca Nacional.

 BIBLIOTECA NACIONAL

Cover Design: Ricardo and Juana Merlo

Library of Congress Cataloging-in-Publication Data

Names: Iolovitch, Marcos, -1984, author. | Blocker, Merrie, translator.
Title: On a clear April morning / Marcos Iolovitch ; translated by Merrie Blocker.
Other titles: Numa clara manhã de abril. English
Description: Boston : Academic Studies Press, 2020. | Series: Jewish Latin American studies | Includes bibliographical references. | Translated into English from Portuguese.
Identifiers: LCCN 2019058058 (print) | LCCN 2019058059 (ebook) | ISBN 9781644692974 (hardback) | ISBN 9781644692981 (paperback) | ISBN 9781644692998 (adobe PDF) | ISBN 9781644693001 (epub)
Subjects: LCSH: Iolovitch, Marcos, -1984--Fiction. | Jews--Brazil--Fiction. | GSAFD: Autobiographical fiction.
Classification: LCC PQ9697.I65 N813 2020 (print) | LCC PQ9697.I65 (ebook) | DDC 869.3/41--dc23
LC record available at https://lccn.loc.gov/2019058058
LC ebook record available at https://lccn.loc.gov/2019058059

Book design by Lapiz Digital Services

Published by Academic Studies Press
1577 Beacon Street
Brookline, MA 02446, USA
www.academicstudiespress.com

*To David, my brother and friend, with my appreciation and gratitude
to all those who suffer and dream of a better world*

Marcos Iolovitch

*To Ana, Damian, Daniela, Juana, Matias, William, Zara, and the little one
on the way, with all my love and caring. May their own journeys bring many
dreams come true.*

Merrie Blocker

Contents

Marcos Iolovitch in Porto Alegre, 1937

Acknowledgements

The publication of this translation and accompanying essays only exists because of the support and kind assistance of so many. First, I want to thank Leo and Tania Iolovitch for entrusting me with the translation of their father's beautiful novel and for sharing so many archival resources. And of course, a warm hug of gratitude to the god-mother of this effort, my good friend Lenora Rosenfield, who introduced me to the Iolovitch family. The god-father of this effort, although his early passing doesn't allow him earthy knowledge of this publication, is Moacyr Scliar, who gave me a copy of this work that had so inspired him, a copy I kept for almost thirty years promising myself that someday I would bring it to the world at large. Moacyr, thank you for this treasure. And, of course, my thanks to Judith Scliar for allowing me to publish my translation of Moacyr's preface to the second Portuguese edition of this novel.

To Professor Regina Igel of the University of Maryland, I send so many thanks for encouraging me when I first thought of translating Marcos Iolovitch's novel and for recommending the translation for publication and for support from the Brazilian National Library's Program for the Translation and Publication of Brazilian Authors. And to Cella and Norman Manea for their continual appreciation for the importance of this translation.

Next, I want to thank Tatiana Ballalai and Isabel Manuela Estrada Portales for helping me assure that this translation was as faithful to Iolovitch's beautiful choice of words and phraseology as it could be. But of course, any errors that remain are my responsibility.

I then want to thank my English language readers who helped me assure that the translation flowed, my friends Diane and Caitlin Fitzgerald, Ellen Sarkisian, and Miki Farcas, my cousin Susan Friedland and my brother and sister Michael Blocker and Elizabeth Ebaugh. To another old friend, Evan Friedman, I send thanks for pointing out to me, not only that Baron Hirsch assisted Jewish farmers in the United States as well as in South America, but that my own grandfather was a recipient of that aid. And to my husband, Ricardo Merlo, I owe many thanks for his daily support throughout this years-long process and his patience as he read out loud endless chapters so I could check that each word and phrase were correctly translated.

To Alessandra Anzani, Darrell Lockhart, and Academic Studies Press, I send my gratitude for believing in the value of this book and for bringing it to publication.

For helping me understand from where this book blossomed and for giving me the information I needed to explain that process to English-language readers, I want to thank the people of the United States and the staffs of the Library of Congress and the US National Archives. It is because the American people truly believe that information should be accessible to all and are willing to invest their tax dollars in that endeavor that I was able to obtain the information included in the preface and afterword. Thank you for giving me and all people from everywhere these opportunities and for making me proud once more of our national values.

For essential support in obtaining primary sources only available in Porto Alegre, I send my gratitude to Anita Bruner and the Marc Chagall Jewish Cultural Institute. I must note that it was Anita who gave me the strength to push forward and find a publisher. When she offered to translate my afterword and publish it in the Marc Chagall Federal University of Rio Grande do Sul web journal *Webmosaica*, I realized this work really mattered.

And I must thank the Brazilian historians Isabel Gritti, Nelson Boeira, and Rene Gertz for sharing their works and for helping me convince myself that my interpretations were indeed valid. I also send to the beyond a warm embrace for my old friend, the historian Sandra Jatahy Pesavento, who also passed away before I began this translation. Reading your works on the intellectual history of Porto Alegre not only gave me crucial information, it allowed me to enjoy once more our sharing of ideas over a *cafezinho*.

To the Brazilian National Library and the Brazilian people who fund this marvelous institution, I send my gratitude for supporting this publication through the Library's Program for the Translation and Publication of Brazilian Authors. To receive this recognition from the preserver of Brazil's literary treasures is a great honor for Mr. Iolovitch, an immigrant from a tiny village in a far off land, who loved his adopted language so much that he didn't just want to give us a story, he wanted to give us Portuguese in all its poetic possibilities.

And finally, and most importantly, I send thanks to the man I have grown to love very much, Marcos Iolovitch. It is because he had such a profound understanding of the human drama, because he had such a deep affection for those near and far, and because he realized that he had an important story to tell, an important addition to our narration of the human experience, that we have been given this piece of history in all its poetry.

Merrie Blocker, Silver Spring, Maryland, February, 2020

Preface to the Second Portuguese Edition by Moacyr Scliar 1987

Within any body of literature there exist some texts that, for some obscure reason, are underestimated. *On a Clear April Morning* falls into this category. Not so much for its literary value, which is appreciable, but which is not reflected in stylistic innovations or flights of imagination. Rather this book's value as a work of documentation is priceless. It speaks to us of an age, it speaks to us of a human experience that decisively marked Judaism and also left an indelible mark on the history of this state, Rio Grande do Sul, and of this country, Brazil. It is about the experience of emigration, an experience that, over the last two thousand years, has not been a rare occurrence in the Jewish timeline. But in this case emigration came with special circumstances.

At the end of the nineteenth century and the beginning of the twentieth, the largest segment of *yishuv*, the world wide Jewish community, lived within the limits of the vast Czarist Empire, in areas especially designated for Jewish settlement. The restriction was not only geographical; it was social and cultural.

Among Jews an aspiration for a better and more dignified existence never disappeared. It was achieved in two ways, through *Aliyah*, to the land of Israel, where the first collective settlements were formed; and by emigration to the New World. America, with its vast expanses of land, its magnificent natural wealth, and its need for labor, opened its doors to the impoverished masses of the Old World. At the entrance to the port of New York the Statue of Liberty (in whose pedestal are engraved the verses of the

Jewish poet Emma Lazarus warmly welcoming the newly arrived) symbolized a guarantee of a life without discrimination or oppression. Millions of Jews came to the United States; a smaller number came to South America.

Here, in the Southern Cone, however, the experience was organized in a unique fashion. The Jewish Colonization Association, a Jewish philanthropic institution, acquired lands in Rio Grande do Sul and Argentina in order to promote Jewish agricultural settlements. But the enterprise did not have the expected success, for numerous reasons—the lack of resources, the inexperience of the emigrants, and the traditional political instability of Latin America, which indeed was directly felt during a bloody revolution in Rio Grande in 1923. All these factors sapped the settlers' spirits and resulted in most of them looking towards the cities.

Then began a new stage in the process, the emigrants' adaptation to the country. It required learning a new language and inserting their group into a society that was already pretty well structured. As can be imagined, it was not easy. Initially it was an arduous path, marked by hard work, by anxiety, and many times by comic or pathetic ventures.

Marcos Iolovitch speaks to us of this path. In his work, as seen only rarely, the man and the writer are one. Marcos, who I knew personally, was a gentle creature, a frail man, but elegant and endowed with a charming kindness. And he wrote exactly like that, with gentleness, with kindness and with elegance. Marcos, like many other intellectuals of his time, was socially engaged. His book of poetry, *Preces Profanas* (*Secular Prayers*), was an attack against injustice and oppression. However, *Preces Profanas* has none of the fierceness of political pamphleteers common among other writers.

On a Clear April Morning has a confessional dimension that can move the most indifferent reader with its innocence and sincerity. Here we have the young emigrant looking with amazed eyes at an unknown country and recording his emotions with absolute fidelity. For example, the scene in which Marcos describes the beginning of his career as a fishmonger is simply a treasure.

Why is this book important for the Brazilian public and especially for the *gaucho* public? Because this is a country of immigrants. Compared with Europeans all of us here are greenhorns. Long-established Brazilians have been in the country four hundred years, in Rio Grande not even that long. That is not enough time for a culture to gel. The Brazilian character is still being formed. As part of this process it is important to record the emigrant experience, but not only as historical facts, statistics, or sociological analyses. It is important to record the emigrant experience as a human phenomenon, as the life of flesh and blood people. This is exactly what Marcos Iolovitch's book does. And the book is even more valuable when we consider how few books of this type we have, particularly those written by talented writers.

As for me, I have a personal debt of gratitude to this book. For me it was what is called an "inspirational" work. I reread it countless times and it never ceased to move me. I paid a small tribute to this work in my first novel *A Guerra no Bom Fim,* not based on the experiences of an emigrant, but rather on the experiences of a son of emigrants. I am very pleased that this tribute no longer refers to an out-of-print book. To recuperate *On a Clear April Morning* for the Brazilian public, the Marc Chagall Institute provides our culture with an invaluable service, and one that also supports well the goals of the Institute itself. But more than this, it pays tribute to the memory of this unforgettable figure, the Jewish-Brazilian writer Marcos Iolovitch.

Translator's Preface

Marcos Iolovitch, author of *On a Clear April Morning,* was an avid student of the great philosophers. But he believed that to reach "true wisdom" we need to open our windows and observe the "subtle shades of reality that envelope" us.[1] In this autobiographical novel, in which a young man seeks to find a righteous and fulfilling path, we watch this charming and caring protagonist discover his own wisdom through the realities that envelop him, the realities of Jewish immigrants in southern Brazil during the first decades of the twentieth century.

As the readers of *On a Clear April Morning* will learn, this story of immigration to Brazil began as a dream for Marcos Iolovitch's father, Yossef, in Zagradowka, a small village one hundred and seventy miles northeast of Odessa in the southern Ukrainian province of Kherson. The publication of this work in English is the fulfillment of a dream that began for me nearly thirty years ago, in Porto Alegre, a small city in Southern Brazil (pop. 1.5 million), five hundred miles south of São Paulo. Porto Alegre, where I served as the public affairs officer in the US Consulate, is the capital of the state of Rio Grande do Sul, home of those that are affectionately called Gaúchos (Gau-oo-chos).

Rio Grande is strongly tied to its European roots as revealed in the faces, surnames, and cuisine alike.[2] A land of immigrants, Germans, Jews, Arabs, Italians, Poles, Portuguese, Rio Grande "has created a . . . peaceful marriage of cultures."[3] It is a place where, as Iolovitch relates, a youngster from a Yiddish speaking family could have as his best friend a son of German immigrants, a place where education could begin in a Jewish "cheder" and later be influenced by Jesuit teachers.

Here you won't find any of Brazil's famed beaches. But you will find, perched on hilltops with breathtaking sunsets over the Guaiba River, a city where civic life, education, and intellectual pursuits matter.

In Porto Alegre, political engagement is a highly held value. It is the capital of a state with only seven percent of the national population, but a state that has given Brazil over twenty percent of its presidents.

Porto Alegre is home to two of Brazil's finest universities, both noted for their teaching and the quantity and excellence of their humanistic and scientific research: the Federal University of Rio Grande do Sul (UFRGS) and the Catholic University of Rio Grande do Sul (PUCRS), rated the best private university in the country.[4]

This translation of *On a Clear April Morning* is the result of the work of another Gaucho center of intellectual inquiry, The Marc Chagall Cultural Institute.[5] Founded in 1985 by Jewish intellectuals and business people, many descendants of immigrants who followed the same path as the Iolovitch family, Instituto Cultural Marc Chagall seeks to preserve and disseminate all aspects of Jewish culture and history. In 1991 the Institute published *Caminhos da esperanca/Pathways of Hope*,[6] a bilingual history of Jews in Rio Grande do Sul. It was written by the critically acclaimed Brazilian Jewish author, Moacyr Scliar, who the New York Times described as "one of Brazil's most celebrated novelists and short-story writers".[7] Moacyr asked me to edit the English text. He also gave me the chance to share his love for Iolovitch's novel, which had inspired his own body of work.

Caminhos da esperanca begins its historical essay with the beautiful opening lines of this novel, "On a clear April morning in the year 19— when the steppes had begun to turn green again upon the joyful entrance of Spring, there appeared scattered about in Zagradowka, a small and cheerful Russian village in the province of Kherson, beautiful brochures with colored illustrations describing the excellent climate, the fertile land, the rich and varied fauna, and the beautiful and exuberant flora, of a vast and far-away country of America, named—BRASIL." And throughout *Caminhos da esperanca* Iolovitch's descriptive prose is cited.

I read *On a Clear April Morning* at one sitting. Delighted by the mixture of lyricism and history that Iolovitch gives us, I wanted the world to have this book. I promised myself that someday I would translate it and obtain its publication in English. That day has finally come.

On a Clear April Morning, first published in 1940, has been recognized by many as the first literary work to draw on the experiences of Russian Jewish immigrants in Brazil. But in the history of Brazilian literature it has an even more important place. As Regina Igel, Coordinator of the Portuguese Program at the University of Maryland, who has spent her life studying the Jewish component in Brazilian literature explains, *On a*

Clear April Morning was "the first [Jewish] needle to penetrate the Brazilian literary fabric . . . [and] was apparently the first novel in Portuguese that draws its subject matter from the Brazilian Jewish community."[8]

As "an inaugural landmark in the [Brazilian] Jewish literary panorama,"[9] and as an historical document depicting the trajectory of early twentieth-century Jewish immigrants to Brazil, *On a Clear April Morning* is indeed worthy of respect. But it is Iolovitch's lyricism, his ability to paint a picture of the emotions and scenes he describes that makes readers fall in love with this book.

Iolovitch's enchanting opening lines that so captivated Scliar have been quoted time and again by those describing Brazilian Jewish or regional literature. But these are only the beginning. *On a Clear April Morning* is full of poetry and often the poetry has musical allusions. Just to cite a few instances: upon departing their Ukrainian village after all the goodbyes, Iolovitch's father's wagon moved down a lonely road as Marcos describes "Chimneys unfolded slow plumes of smoke in the chilly morning air. In concert, the cadence of a distant engine and the rhythmic fall of a hammer upon an anvil accompanied the slow ascent of the day. . . . "

Or when he fell in love, Marcos laments the object of his heart that is many miles away: "Her image never left me, not for a second. I saw her in everything and everywhere. She was on the page of the book that I opened, on the blank sheets of paper that I touched, in the paleness of the moon, and in the brilliance of the stars."

Or when his poverty forces him to live in a leaky newspaper-lined shed, he communes with the "drops of water [that] began to beat to the rhythm of the rain. . . .

Little droplet, little droplet, I murmured, how sad is your muffled tempo. . . , your sad cadence. . . . "

On a Clear April Morning is full of poetry and musical cadences and tempos because Marcos Iolovitch was both a musician and a poet. He supported himself by teaching the violin for several years. And poetry was his real literary love. *On a Clear April Morning* is Iolovitch's only full-length narrative work. His two other books *Eu e Tu* (I and Thou) published in 1932 and *Preces Profanas* (Secular Prayers) published in 1949 are collections of poems and poetical aphorisms.

As do so many young poets, this sensitive young man used his pen to understand humanity and the meaning of life. As he describes, the first years in Brazil did not fulfill his father's dream. Instead they were full of hunger, tragic deaths, economic failures, anti-Semitism, and his father's alcoholic response. "Why and for what do we live?" Iolovitch asks. Why does God "distribute rewards and punishments without even the most basic concern for equality and justice"?

He seeks his answers in the great nineteenth- and early twentieth-century philosophers, in the realm of the intellect where one of his favorite philosophers, Arthur Schopenhauer, noted, " pain has no power."[10] Iolovitch dedicates a whole chapter of *On a Clear April Morning* to Schopenhauer. And he most likely took the title of his first book, *I and Thou* from the best-known treatise of the great Jewish philosopher, Martin Buber. In *I and Thou*, Iolovitch reflects the concept that Buber develops in his *I and Thou* that "man becomes whole not in relation to himself but only through relation to another self".[11]

In Buber the true I-Thou relationship is that "in which two persons face and accept each other as truly human."[12] This acceptance of each person as truly human and the compassion that results is what defined Iolovitch. Moacyr Scliar describes him as "endowed with a charming kindness."[13]

Iolovitch was kind because he cared about others. Even when he was wronged, he saw his aggressors as human beings. Instead of becoming vengeful he tried to understand them. After being attacked by anti-Semitic bullies, for example, he realizes that their anger towards Jews was not an inherent evil. Rather it was the result of some priests who taught their students the most incredible lies about Jews. Instead of bringing to their students the commandment to "love thy neighbor as preached by Christ, they brought the seeds of hate. . . . "

As a child Iolovitch's greatest pain came from "the tears of my mother and my two brothers. . . , " caused by his father's drinking. But even then, he understood that his father was a "good man [who drank because] it hurt him to see the family reduced to such a deplorable state." As he grows, Iolovitch's compassion reaches further. He dedicated *On a Clear April Morning* to "all those who suffer and dream of a better world."

In 1940 an interviewer wrote, "Marcos is a great idealist, a passionate dreamer that takes very seriously human existence and he is totally sincere when he says that his wish is for a better world for all humanity."[14] He was inspired by authors that "elevated mankind, that dignified the human species, that ennobled life."[15] And that is what he attempted in *On a Clear April Morning*. He describes the nobility of his everyday characters, as in his brother's efforts to build a pushcart so they can peddle fish, or in an older couple's efforts to enliven the life of a young child from a poor family with trips to an unknown paradise, the movie house.

But after the Second World War and all its horrors Iolovitch becomes a very frustrated idealist. His final book, *Preces Profanas* (1949), is a protest to the Lord for the suffering of all mankind, "Jews, Catholics, the Muslims, and Buddhists, the believers and nonbelievers, the saints and the sinners."[16]

Like most literary works, *On a Clear April Morning* was not created in an intellectual vacuum. Since the 1890s Rio Grande do Sul had been Brazil's most literate state and by the 1920s Porto Alegre "already possessed . . . important books stores, cinemas, newspapers and an active intellectual life . . . [with] dozens of published authors."[17] This city of immigrants was enriched by a European concern for ideas and enjoyed European resources. Often Germany was the source.[18] Twenty percent of the state was German-born or descendants of German immigrants. Various bookstores sold works in German and German Jesuits were instrumental in supporting the study of philosophy in both Catholic and secular educational institutions, including those that Iolovitch and his friends attended.[19]

German most likely presented Marcos with few difficulties. Even early on Iolovitch's family, like probably many of the Jewish immigrants, had found comfort in Rio Grande's German roots. When a nurse of German descent needed to explain to Marco's father that the nine-year-old boy had typhoid fever, she had no problem. Yiddish, the language of Eastern European Jews, is descended from a medieval German dialect.

But most important for writers, Porto Alegre was the home of one of Brazil's most dynamic publishing houses, Editora Globo, and its noted literary journal, *Revista do Globo*.

Editora Globo sought the newest in literature and offered the chance to publish to many young writers. As a result, in the 1930s and 40s Rio Grande do Sul gave Brazil some of its most important authors. Each one "reached out to a different sector of reality seeking to convey it with his own personal vision." These authors often described "human beings whose living conditions were far from ideal," and often designed plots that addressed philosophical, political, and social issues.[20] They had a cultural conscience. They were concerned with principles, with goodness and sought to balance intellectual and psychological concerns.[21] And in some works, the lyricism was extreme.[22]

Iolovitch fit right in. Of course, he chose his topic from the sector he knew best, the Jewish community. He explored principles and included intellectual and psychological concerns in his work. He filled *On a Clear April Morning* with discussions on the origins of anti-Semitism, the misguided paths mankind chooses, and the injustices of society but always beautified by his poetry and lightened by the ironies of Jewish humor.

In addition to Schopenhauer and Buber, Iolovitch and his friends read many of the nineteenth-century sages including Charles Darwin,

Herbert Spencer, Auguste Comte, Ernst Haeckel, Ludwig Buchner, and Jean-Baptiste Lamarck. They were searching for a rational and scientific explanation of the cosmic and societal phenomena that surrounded them. They also read the moderns. Iolovitch listed among his favorites Erich Maria Remarque, Andre Gide, Aldous Huxley, Somerset Maugham, and Guillame Apollinaire.[23]

But it was probably Leo Tolstoy that most influenced *On a Clear April Morning*. In an interview at the time of this novel's first publication in 1940, Iolovitch notes that during the previous ten years he had been continually reading Tolstoy's early autobiographical novels, *Childhood, Boyhood, and Youth*.[24] Iolovitch must have been inspired by Tolstoy's great powers of detailed pictorial observations that so mirrored his own. He must have felt a warm sense of companionship as he watched Tolstoy's protagonist, like Iolovitch himself and the protagonist he will create in *On a Clear April Morning*, struggle with ethical concerns, sexual awakening, and religious doubts.

Like Tolstoy, Iolovitch began his novel with a dateless moment: Iolovitch—"On a clear April morning in the year 19…"; Tolstoy—"On the 12th of August, 18**."[25] Both writers used these vague historical moments because these young authors, although drawing on their own experiences, sought to write universal tales of growing up. They sought to write tales filled with youth's desire to understand the world, to assess morality, and to find a path for a righteous and valued life. To create this universality, they didn't write autobiographies but used the autobiographical form that allows insertion of fictional elements and permits the author to choose "experiences which transform and mold a character."[26]

Tolstoy of course went on to write many more tales. Unfortunately, especially for those enthralled with *On a Clear April Morning's* beautiful prose, Iolovitch did not.

In the 1930s and 40s Iolovitch was a recognized member of the Gaucho literary world. His short stories and poems appeared in the prestigious *Revista do Globo*. When southern Brazilian literature was discussed, his name was included along with those whose fame still resonates today. He appears in numerous dictionaries of Brazilian and Latin American writers. He was interviewed on the front page of a major newspaper.[27] The Brazilian pavilion at the 1939–40 World Fair in New York displayed his books. And Iolovitch formed part of Rio Grande do Sul's delegation to one of Brazil's most important cultural events of the twentieth century, the first Brazilian Writers Congress, held in São Paulo in 1945.[28] But after the publication of *Preces Profanas* in 1949, his writing seems to have ceased. Instead, perhaps because of his new responsibilities as a father, he dedicated himself to his legal practice. He never made much money but then he didn't love the law. He had chosen legal studies because he needed to work his way through school and the law school didn't require class attendance, just successful final exams.

But just before Iolovitch ceased writing, a ten-year-old boy wrote him a letter extolling the beauty of Iolovitch's poems in *Preces Profanas*, "one of the most beautiful books I have ever read."[29] That young boy grew up to be the noted author Moacyr Scliar who arranged for the second edition of *Numa Clara Manha de Abril* to be published in 1987 and passed the book to me. To Moacyr, the "god-father" of this English edition who I often felt guided its formation from on high (Moacyr passed away prematurely in 2011) I send my deepest gratitude. Because Moacyr believed so much in the inspirational beauty of Iolovitch's novel, English-language readers will now have their own chance to fall in love with *On a Clear April Morning*.

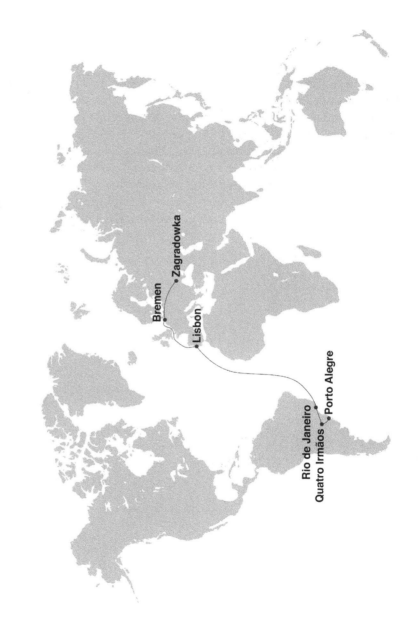

Marcos' Journey

Zagradowka

Bremen

Lisbon

Rio de Janeiro
Quatro Irmãos
Porto Alegre

Chapter 1

On a clear April morning in the year 19… when the steppes had begun to turn green again upon the joyful entrance of Spring, there appeared scattered about in Zagradowka, a small and cheerful Russian village in the province of Kherson, beautiful brochures with colored illustrations describing the excellent climate, the fertile land, the rich and varied fauna, and the beautiful and exuberant flora, of a vast and faraway country of America, named—BRASIL where the "Jewish Colonization Association," better known as the JCA, owner of a great parcel of land, called "Quatro Irmãos," located in the municipality of Boa Vista do Erechim, in the state of Rio Grande do Sul, was offering homesteads on favorable terms to all those who wished to become farmers.

Situated on the left bank of the Schisterni River, on whose bed the village youth used to skate in winter when the waters transformed themselves into a thick and polished mass of ice, Zagradowka lay far from civilization, forgotten by the world, abandoned by the government and left to its own fate, as were innumerable small communities of the extinct Czarist Empire that found themselves dispersed across the immeasurable vastness of the steppes.

Zagradowka's inhabitants, simple, uneducated, and unrefined people, lived peacefully from trade and agriculture.

A wide central street, crossed by various narrow lanes, divided the village in half. Almost at the end of the street, where it opened up into two roads that led towards the different *linhas coloniais*,[1] there arose in the center of a circular garden a little church. At the entrance to the village, on the right-hand side for someone coming from the river, was my father's commercial establishment. And, on the same side, at the other end of the street, near the church, was the business belonging to his stepfather, the oldest and wealthiest wheat merchant in that region, with whom my grandmother had entered into second nuptials three years after the death of her first husband.

Orphaned at eight years of age, my father began to work in his stepfather's establishment. He spent his adolescence at the counter, accumulating some savings in exchange. When he was nineteen, he married, opening a modest store of his own.

With an open nature and a deeply caring heart, he enjoyed widespread esteem among his fellow countrymen and an almost carefree life. When the shelves emptied a bit and needed new wares, he would go by sleigh to Krivoy Rog to make the necessary purchases. And so, his life glided along placidly, always maintaining the same rhythm, without any bumps in the road.

But, with the passing years and the coming of children, he began to worry about their future.

Reading the brochures roused the villagers from their usual tranquility, provoking absurd comments on the validity of the information and the true geographic location of Brazil. From that day on no one spoke of anything else. It was *the* topic everywhere. In the pharmacy, in the stores, in the synagogue, and, especially, at the weekly Friday market.

Some inhabitants of Zagradowka were not unaware of the existence of a free and fabulously wealthy land called America, though they had only formed a vague and nebulous image of this faraway place. But they had never heard of Brazil. In their eyes, Brazil was just a legend, created by the imagination of some adventurers.

Papa also had little education, but he had no doubts about the truth of the offerings. He had complete trust in the goodness of mankind. That's why he read and reread these brochures with growing interest. And he ended up vividly enraptured by the description of this new land. Especially by the colored illustration on the cover.

The cover of the brochures displayed a simple landscape depicting rural Brazilian life.

Under a clear and distant soft blue sky, a farmer, with a wide-brimmed hat and a white shirt with rolled-up sleeves, was bent over, wielding the handles of a plow pulled by a team of oxen turning over the virgin land. A little farther on, in the background, lay the golden crop, extensive ripe wheat fields. Even further back, blued in the distance, were coconuts, palms, and mysterious forests. And, in the foreground, highlighted in vivid and bold colors, was an enormous orchard, composed principally of orange trees; in their shade pigs ate the beautiful oranges that had fallen to the ground.

This little picture impressed Papa profoundly.

He didn't like trade, the exploitation of naïve peasants. Agriculture, however, seduced him. It was reputed to be one of the cleanest and most honorable professions. That's why he wanted his children, who were all boys, to pursue it. He deemed that he could assure them a splendid future by making them farmers. With time, he thought, they would marry. They would form a large family. They would all live together, leading a happy life in a tranquil corner of a virgin world.

He saw in Brazil the heaven-sent land for the realization of his plans.

For some time, he secreted this beautiful dream deep inside him. He didn't let himself reveal it to anyone. He spent his spare time contemplating the colorful cover and the orange trees.

Oranges in Russia were imported. They came packed in boxes and rolled in tissue paper like the apples from California here in Brazil. And they were very expensive.

Papa would look at the wheat field, at this symbol of abundance. He imagined himself a grand farmer, tilling the soil with his sons, far away, very far away, in a distant land called Brazil.

Finally, having resolved to change his life, he shared with his wife his resolution to leave Russia to become a farmer in the New World.

Mama energetically opposed this plan, invoking heartfelt concerns. She wasn't going to leave her family and friends to go adventuring in a land whose existence she doubted. But her objections did not dissuade him. And soon after, to make his decision irrevocable, he put his business up for sale. He sold all that he had. And he set the departure date.

On the appointed day, with farewells and embraces, the whole town came to wish us a successful journey.

My brothers and I were seated on a wagon crammed full with baggage while my parents said goodbye.

With great difficulty, they managed to disentangle themselves from their friends and family and their deeply felt embraces. Eyes brimming with tears, they pressed to their hearts each one there, trying, in vain, to hide their premonition that each one of those embraces would be the last they would share this side of heaven.

The farewells completed, my parents sat down on the coach-box of the wagon as it slowly began to move.

Repressed sobs erupted from those beloved friends. Wailing spread everywhere. Both men and women lowered their heads wiping their eyes. Various hats and handkerchiefs waved in the morning light.

Some relatives began to follow us at a distance while the vehicle moved on slowly, leaving behind two parallel grooves on the straight and seldom followed road which stretched out like a dark ribbon until falling out of sight in the shallow flatness of the fields.

Only many, many years afterward did I come to understand the significance of two parallel lines. . . .

After having covered some distance, Papa turned to look back at his native village for the last time.

The crowd of friends and family had dispersed. The town remained behind, way behind.

Chimneys unfolded slow plumes of smoke in the chilly morning air. In concert, the cadence of a distant engine and the rhythmic fall of a hammer upon an anvil accompanied, synchronically, the billowing ascent of the day, which the sun had been flooding with the joy of its light. Like the wing of an injured bird, a single handkerchief moved slowly in the air.

Who would have stayed there waving to him, always from the same place?

To see better, he squinted his eyes a bit.

It was a handkerchief, blowing in the wind, that someone had left stuck in a bush, giving the impression that the steppe itself, which had seen him born and, now, was seeing him leave for an uncertain destiny, was wishing him its ultimate goodbye with the silent eloquence of its sad wave. . . .

Chapter 2

Of our uncomfortable journey as second-class passengers through the different European countries we crossed, I retain only vague reminiscences, like the confused and indistinct images of dreams that don't leave any clear traces in your consciousness.

Muted impressions of train transfers. Of dust that rose from the roads. Of locomotive smoke. Of a rapid and infinite succession of richly varied landscapes galloping past in a whirl. Impressions of frenetic and tumultuous activity in Bremen, the German port, jammed with tankers, boats, tugs, and steamers. Impressions of piers crammed with bundles, bags, and boxes with stevedores and cranes feverishly loading and unloading ships, building heaps of baggage and piles of goods. Impressions of emigrant quarters filled with a confused babel of people, races, and languages.

But from the ocean crossing, I retain sharper impressions.

Thirty-two days of a sea journey, in the foul and gloomy bottom of a cargo ship, don't fade away easily from your soul.

After a short stay in Bremen, we were taken, along with eleven more Jewish families who were also emigrating to Brazil, on board a freighter that was leaving for South America because we had missed the passenger ship that should have brought us here.

A thick mist enveloped the port, diluting the ashen and compact mass of heavy and steadily illuminated buildings. As we got closer to the pier the city disappeared more and more into the distance into a dense fog that gave the port a submarine cast, colorless, almost immaterial, as if life had returned in a split second to the most distant eras, those that preceded the miraculous word of creation, as if the world had been plunged into its original primordial chaos.

Treading the shifting planks of the gangway that led us from the pier to the ship, I trembled with fear. The sea below was hideous, resembling a fabulous roaring monster, furious that he was not able to swallow us up. Papa, who had been holding onto me, held me even tighter.

One by one the sailors made us descend a vertical iron ladder to a dark hold that gave off a suffocating smell of fresh paint.

Two rows of bunk beds formed a common dormitory for thirty-eight passengers. In an adjoining space was the dining hall.

The emigrants, anxious to secure good places, invaded the hold, creating much confusion and a deafening commotion. The men were pushing, elbowing their way through, dragging children behind them. Women called out for their husbands. Some scolded their crying children, adding loud curses to the general bedlam. Other women, who had already found places, were seated on their suitcases or on the edges of the beds with their limp white breasts exposed as they fanned themselves and nursed the children.

"Stay here," bellowed one woman, shouting at a sobbing child whose eyes were reddened from weeping. "Your place is here, damn you! If you go up there again, I'll cut your head off, by Satan I will. . . . Did you hear? Cut . . . your . . . head . . . off. . . . "

The young boy cowered in fear as if he already felt on his little neck the sharp edge of the guillotine. He was crazy to be on deck, to see the ocean. To see the waves rolling in the darkness and the city retreating and disappearing, bit by bit, into the distance.

The process of securing places provoked discussions, protests, complaints. And every so often there were damning outcries. But little by little the voices were quieting. Everyone found places and calm was being restored.

The women put the children to sleep and tried to get comfortable themselves. Some men found some decks of cards and went to play in the dining hall. Others, lying down with their hands clasped behind their necks, with eyes fastened on the ceiling, were smoking pensively or conversing with their bunkmates. A lamp dangling from the center of the ceiling shed a sad, mournful light on this cramped compartment in which were housed twelve families, like captives on a slave ship.

That night I lowered myself from the bed where I had been laid, got up on a chair and looked out through the porthole.

A dreadful endless darkness enveloped the space. Mountainous breakers exploded against the ship's hull, rocking it with intense ferocity.

We were in the open sea where the sky and the water unite in that most impressive cosmic communion from which mankind draws the tragic idea of the universe's infinite grandeur.

Frightened, I moved away from the little circular window and returned to bed, pulling the cover over my head.

The ship tilted towards the bow and then towards the stern, casting the passengers backward and forwards, rhythmically. The suitcases and packages that were on the floor drifted back and forth to the same tempo accompanied by the monotonous pulse of the engines' muffled gasps.

The violence of the sea grew stronger. Enormous surging waves smashed against the ship, tipping it to the right. Here the ship stayed for a few seconds and then slowly regained its balance. Once it was level, it brusquely tipped to the left and shortly thereafter tilted again to the right. Then once more to the left, with redoubled speed. And so successively without cessation, the ship was painfully overcoming the resistant force of the swirling waters that rocked the vessel with growing momentum, while stirring up the bowels of its passengers.

A sensation of nausea made me uncover my head. Everyone was indisposed. Some already felt very sick.

"Jaco," a woman called softly. And then afterward louder, "Jaco!"

"What is it?" grumbled her husband.

"I'm not feeling well."

"And what do you want me to do?"

"Ay," moaned the woman writhing, with her head outside the bunk and her opened mouth turned downwards.

She was pale, her face contorted.

Her husband supported her head and tried to encourage her.

"Calm down . . . calm down . . . this will pass."

"Jaco," she exclaimed, twitching all over with her hand on her belly. But she couldn't finish.

A gush of nauseating liquid spread out over the floor. Then came another one. And then another. The woman sat up colorless with her eyes watering from the convulsions, almost breathless. Sticky threads of vomit trickled from her mouth. She cleaned herself and took a little of the water that her husband brought her. Then she leaned back on the pillow, moaning.

Other passengers also felt their stomachs turn. Those that were in the dining hall, playing cards, abandoned their games and wobbled back to the sleeping quarters, supporting themselves on the bunk railings.

In a corner of the hall, a boy vomited from an upper bunk, pouring out thick disgusting streams.

The atmosphere in the dormitory was no longer fit to breathe. A rancid smell filled the air.

Armed with brooms and dumping out buckets of water, sailors cleaned the room while joking with the travelers.

Papa soon managed to get us out of the hold and found us spots on the ship's deck.

The free fresh sea air revived us immediately. And we got through the night more or less all right. But at daybreak, the seamen came to wash the deck obliging us to go down into the hold, and they repeated this every morning. Even so, we preferred sleeping under open skies. Only on rainy nights did we stay below.

The first days of the trip, although quite revolting, passed quickly. But the following ones were harder to get through. They were long and very boring. Always the same seascape. Above, sky and water. And below in the hold, people vomiting. With the passing of time, however, the passengers became more and more used to the tossing sea and managed to lighten the voyage with some distractions.

One of the men's favorite amusements and one that was also enjoyed a lot by the women and children consisted of having a man stand facing the wall, with his back to the others. He covered his eyes with one of his hands and put the other hand palm up on his behind which faced his fellow passengers who were arranged in a semi-circle. One of them slapped his hand. Then the victim had to immediately turn around and identify the perpetrator. If he made a mistake, he had to stand facing the wall again and receive further slaps until he guessed correctly. And once the identity of the slapper was discovered, he took his victim's place.

Those with less expertise received many blows, immensely delighting the spectators.

Sometimes a sailor, who was feared for his robust constitution, participated in this game. He didn't manage to hit more than once because he was immediately identified by the weight of his wrist. But even this one slap was felt for quite a long time because he used his strength to strike with an excessive force that outraged our fellow passengers.

When my father, whose physical vigor was also respected, found out about these complaints against the sailor, he took advantage of a turn that placed him behind the seaman and gave him such a thunderous blow that this playful game nearly degenerated into a fight.

Other passengers immediately intervened, and Papa and the sailor were reconciled. From that day on, the sailor comported himself with greater moderation whenever he joined the game.

This and other distractions eased the passage of our days. But the nights were always very long and very sad. They seemed interminable. The roar of the sea brought us dark thoughts that took away our sleep. Anguished, we awaited the morning's dawn, counting the minutes. And time drained away with the unbearable slow motion of true torture.

The women spent their days complaining of the food and the swaying sea. Many damned the hour they had abandoned the tranquility of their homes in search of a better future. One went on and on, nagging her husband so he would persuade the captain to halt the steamship for a few moments.

"Tell him to stop," she begged, "I can't stand the throws of this rough sea any longer."

"Don't you see that it is impossible for him to do that?" her husband reasoned in a soft voice, to make her understand the absurdity of her request.

"Why impossible?" she retorted heatedly. "What's impossible is for me to continue this damn voyage. I can't eat or sleep. I'm wasting away, more each day. I don't think I'll arrive at the first port alive. Why this hurry? Go and tell this bandit to stop, if only for a half hour."

It goes without saying that her husband didn't comply with her request and so his wife continued to implore him with the most whopping damnations, as the language of the Jews is very rich.

And like this many days went by.

One morning all the passengers flocked to the deck and anxiously scanned the wide, empty horizon. They had been informed the night before that on this day they would arrive in Portugal.

The waters had been growing calmer since the previous evening. Cheerful flocks of sea gulls were circling overhead. They had come to announce that land was near. All of a sudden, an enthusiastic cry shook the air.

"Land . . . land," shouted a man with his hand pointing at the horizon.

All stretched their eyes towards the direction he indicated.

Far off, very far off, a dark spot almost invisibly began to appear on the clear blue expanse.

Greater delight, for sure, not even Columbus' mates had felt when four hundred years before they had sighted the New World.

The facial expressions that had been extinguished by long nights of seasickness and wakefulness revived themselves as if by a miracle, radiating intense happiness. The women cried with joy, embracing their husbands. The oldest among us put their hands together and prayed. Everyone shared the excitement.

Slow, slowly the dark spot was growing and taking on contours. And shortly afterward standing out sharply against the dimmed blue of the sky, appeared the angular lines of a gigantic urban silhouette.

It was Lisbon.

From the tops of the narrow towers of Belem, the bells sent us festive fraternal greetings from the old and historic Lusitanian capital. And after a short stay in Portuguese waters, we continued.

From Lisbon to Brazil, the voyage was much smoother and more interesting.

From time to time islands lost in the ocean's vastness emerged from the waters like verdant nests. With pity, we looked on the isolated and limited lives of the inhabitants of these islands.

At one of them, we stopped.

Semi-naked men and children circled our ship with small boats, waiting for us to throw coins into the water. Then they would collect them from the bottom of the sea. In this maneuver, they showed extraordinary skill. A nickel was thrown into the water, and a swimmer would dive into the spot where it landed, disappearing for a few moments. Then he would return, carrying the coin sparkling in his white teeth.

The arrival in Rio de Janeiro was a feast of light and color.

Captivated, everyone beheld the marvelous tropical city in Guanabara Bay, which looked so happy at that early morning hour as if it were in love with its own charms.

With languid and measured movements, the waters wove a broad white lace of foam to cloak the elegant nudity of the beach's sensual curves.

An agent of the colonization association, whose secretary I would become years later in Porto Alegre, came to receive us, taking us to the Isle of Flowers where we would stay for some days, recovering from the long and arduous sea journey.

Chapter 3

From the Isle of Flowers, we continued to Erebango in Boa Vista do Erechim, our final destination.

Of this last stage of our journey I have no memory apart from the cold and rainy night we arrived in Erebango where we were picked up by a settler who lodged us in his house until the day the immigrant barracks, then under construction, were finished.

One of the first visits we received in the new land was from Death who carried away forever my youngest brother.

My parents had gone to visit a family that lived at quite a distance, and they had taken him with them. Returning, they went the wrong way and got lost in the woods, where they were forced to pass the night. The following morning when they arrived home, the child was feverish. Days later he passed away.

I still remember well the day of his death.

Seated in the yard on a pine log, Mama cried. Near her, letting heavy tears fall silently over the boards he was nailing, Papa was making the funeral coffin for his dead son. Each time he put a nail into the wood it was as if he were burying it in his own heart. At a little distance, without understanding, my brother Daniel and I observed that painful picture.

Mama called us. She embraced us. She squeezed us tightly against her heart, hugging us close. And after covering us with kisses mixed with tears, she raised her eyes to the pristine, serene sky and sent a fervent plea, asking God to spare us.

The coffin ready, we placed the corpse inside. Luiz, the oldest of my brothers, mounted the horse and Papa brought the casket bearing a piece of his life that was leaving to be buried.

Once Luiz started for the cemetery, which was very far away, Mama's laments burst out even stronger. With loud cries she called for her son, exclaiming,

"Don't take my boy. . . . My sweet little one, my darling, why are you leaving your poor mother?"

Papa hugged her and took her inside the house. Both took off their thongs, sat down on the hard-beaten dirt floor, their chests swaying back and forth, and began to pray, intoning in Hebrew the saddest song I ever heard in my life, the old funeral chant of our people.

We were moved to the immigrant shelter once the sacramental days of mourning, part of the Jewish funeral ritual, were finished.

This was a wooden barrack that sheltered, under its ceilingless roof, eight families, more or less. It had no real interior divisions. Rather, these were made with sheets that the occupants stretched out in the guise of walls so they would have a pale illusion of privacy.

But communal life in the shelter wasn't always sad.

One night, a baby about a year old, awakened in the darkness by hunger, set out to find the breast of his mother who slept at his side. And by mistake, he raised his greedy little mouth to the bosom of a young maiden. Feeling the voluptuous pressure of lips on her chest, she let out an instinctive shout that woke up the whole shelter.

This mistake shows the great space that separated the occupants at night.

We waited for the demarcation of our homestead for many months. And while we waited, we were spending what was left of our meager savings, since the trip from Russia had been at our expense.

When the day we took possession of our lands arrived, we boarded a wagon pulled by a pair of horses and headed out.

The day was gloomy, threatening to rain.

As we reached the main road, a strong downpour burst out, drowning a brood of chicks that we were carrying in a pail hung from the back of the vehicle.

Papa came to sit in the front of the wagon to guide the animals. At his side, curled up and silent was Mama.

As the rain stopped, the clouds frayed, giving a glimpse of washed patches of sky. And the sun reappeared, spreading the joy of a recovered patient over the wet fields.

After many hours of travel, we entered a forest by a narrow trail, recently opened. At a certain point, I don't know why, the horses were frightened and took off, unbridled, threatening to turn over the vehicle at any moment, which miraculously remained upright.

Mama threw herself to the back, grabbing us, while Papa pulled the reins, shouting, "Hold up, hold up. . . . "

Birds fled in terror. Reptiles quickly crossed the road and hid deep in the woods. Whizzing branches that had been spread out on the road pounded our heads and faces.

When we reached a small incline in the middle of a field on the other side of the forest, the horses were obliged to stop. During their flight, we had lost a basket full of sweet buns brought from Russia. Later on, we truly regretted this loss because the bread that the settlement gave us was quite bitter. . . .

We rested a little, and then we continued our trek, arriving at our destination a little before nightfall.

Various men, seated around some wooden logs burning over a handful of charcoal embers, were sipping mate tea that they passed from one to another.

Not knowing how to speak Brazilian, Papa greeted them with a timid flick of the head to which all responded. Right away, a dark-skinned half-breed, with a thin graying beard and a gentle gaze that inspired confidence, stood up and came to shake our hands.

Papa gave him a letter from the company's management, which presented the bearer as the owner of the lands this dark-skinned man occupied.

After reading the letter, the man pointed to a place near the fire. The circle in front of the pan of embers opened up a little, to give us some space. And the men resumed the conversation that had been interrupted by our arrival.

One of the hands unhitched the animals and carried our baggage to the shed.

Night was falling.

In the sanguine sunset, the afternoon shed its last glow. The first shadows leaving the valleys and the wetlands dragged themselves through the rolling grasslands and slowly covered the hills. A great silence, slightly broken by the gurgling murmur of a nearby brook, by the doleful peeps of lost birds, and by the harmonic dissonance of buzzing insects and croaking frogs, rose from the ground, shedding a soft, deep, and solemn peace over the melancholy loneliness of the fields.

Finally, we were in possession of our lands.

After a few days, the previous occupant of these lands gathered his men and belongings and went in search of another perch.

The rustic laborers left first, driving a passel of hogs and a herd of cattle. Their boss was the last to go, leaving us a pretty dog to remember him by.

On this homestead, we spent three years of great privation. Of hard experiences. Of attempts and failures. And we were beaten in our fight against the soil; each one of us receiving our own baptism by blood.

As the result of falling off a horse, Davi broke one arm. Solon cut himself on the foot with an unfortunate blow of an ax. Papa was injured by an ox. Myself, I was almost torn apart by a diamond-shaped harrow with teeth of iron, guiding a team of oxen as we broke up the clods of dirt left on the plowed ground. Even today I still have an enormous scar on my left shoulder. And the indelible memory of this accident.

We didn't know how to tame the cattle that were portioned out to us or how to till the land. And the result was a true disaster.

But my saddest recollection from our life as failed farmers was the loss of another little brother.

It was a tepid summer afternoon.

I was in the corral collecting the stiff hair the animals had left on the barbed wire which I used to braid reins for my little wooden horses.

Since the previous evening, we had been awaiting the return of my parents who had gone by cart with our youngest brother to the district seat to visit our neighbor who was sick in the hospital.

All of a sudden, I saw in the distance two figures walking, followed by a cart. In spite of the distance, I recognized them right away. I left my toys and ran to meet them. But as I drew nearer, my joy transformed itself into sad misgiving.

Supported by Papa and with unsure steps, Mama approached, crying. And both were soaked, their clothes sticking to their bodies.

"You lost another brother," Mama said sobbing, without even hugging me.

Only then did I notice the absence of my little brother.

The closer Mama got to the house, the more she lost her strength. Going up a small hill she fainted. Papa took her in his arms. He laid her down in the bedroom. And he sprayed her face with water mixed with vinegar.

When she came to, she became delirious, calling for her son. That was when I learned how the disaster had happened.

Coming back from the hospital, as they were just crossing the last small bridge, the oxen were frightened and overturned the cart. With her son on her lap, Mama fell into the river. It happened so quickly that Papa barely had time to jump out of the vehicle and watch his wife and son being swallowed up by the water. Then, for a few seconds, that sight left him on the bridge, utterly petrified, like an immobile statue.

Feeling herself pulled by the waters, as the current was strong under the small bridge, Mama, in an instinctive defensive gesture, raised her arms, grabbing onto one of the branches that brushed the river's surface. Seeing her fighting with death, Papa threw himself into the river and managed to save her even though she had faded away. When she regained consciousness, they realized their son was gone.

In desperation, they vainly searched for him. The impetuous flow of the waters had dragged him far away—very, very far.

Faced with Mama's growing delirium and staggering screams as she called for her son, my oldest brothers went to the site of the fatality to try again. And for many hours they searched without success for the drowned body, churning through the waters surrounding the bridge, in all directions, following the river's flow. Finally, having lost all hope, they returned home.

Mama was sleeping. At her side, his elbows jammed on his knees, his head held in his hands, Papa sat watch. A mournful silence enveloped everything. No one spoke. With just a look we understood each other.

Luiz decided that we should sleep in the shed.

It was a clear and somewhat warm night. Through a wide crack in the shed, I saw come out of the woods a semicircular brilliance, adorned with a pale golden halo, ascending and expanding slowly until it took the form of an enormous red-colored disk.

It was the moon.

"Look how pretty the moon is!" I exclaimed in Yiddish.

"Today we mustn't think anything pretty," Luiz warned me.

But even so, I couldn't take my eyes away from the moon. And I continued to watch it until I fell asleep.

On the next day, very early, my brothers returned to search for the cadaver.

Under the fateful little bridge and nearby, the river's bed was probed everywhere, without any result. Realizing that their efforts were useless, my brothers gave up the search. And in their treacherous bed, the waters forever kept my brother's little body.

But, days after the disaster, to console Mama, Papa and Luiz convinced her that they had found him by chance, floating on the surface of a river, lost in a far-off forest, while they were stretching some barbed wire nearby. And as the place they were referring to was very far from home and the cadaver was now in an advanced state of decomposition, they had buried him near that river.

To soothe her, it was necessary to invent this lie. She couldn't accept the painful idea that even after death, her son would have no rest and instead would be perpetually dragged by the waters, serving as feed for the fish and the vultures.

I too was naïve. I assumed that there was no greater suffering than my mother's. But when I became a man life showed me I had been deceived.

And truly, oh Mother, how small is your suffering compared to the suffering of those unhappy mothers who, beaten down by misery, see the live flesh of their daughters devoured many times with impunity by the vultures and sharks that fill the great river of life. . . !

Chapter 4

Felled by these setbacks, defeated by the lack of farming experience, we suffered extreme shortages. Our food supplies were reduced to yucca flour and sweet potatoes.

Left to us as a last resort was hunting. But that is prohibited by the Jewish faith that only allows the consumption of meat under the rigorous observance of the rituals prescribed by its laws. Food prepared according to these dietary rules is called "kosher." And "treif" is the name given to food prepared in violation of those rules.

My father was religious, as still are most of the Jews of the older generation. For this reason, he preferred to endure hunger rather than transgress one of the precepts of his centuries-old faith. But to spare his children the dire consequences of his religious beliefs, he resolved to abandon farming, and become a day laborer, as did my oldest brother.

In the beginning, they earned a living as members of a crew building a railroad. Then they went to work for the company, JCA. They fenced the homesteads with barbed wire. They dug holes. They planted stakes. And they nailed the wire.

If I am not mistaken, they realized a dime for the opening of each pit, measuring two feet in depth and ten inches in diameter.

They left for work in the early morning on Mondays and only returned on Fridays at nightfall to spend Saturday at home, the day of rest for the Jews.

With tools on their shoulders and knapsacks on their backs, carrying the provisions for an entire week of arduous labor, a kettle, a loaf of yucca bread, a little coffee, and some sugar, and their legs bandaged with strips of cloth cut from burlap sacks with their feet rolled up in bags of the same fabric, they left home, wife, children and brothers and set out for the harsh battle for a piece of bread, like two men condemned to forced labor. Carrying in their souls the resigned sorrow of the defeated and in their hearts the uncertainty of return, they made their way through the woods, wallowing through the bogs, to open holes in the hard earth of the fields.

They worked from sunup to sundown, exposed to the elements, sleeping out in the cold. They returned always exhausted, filthy, their clothes grimy with red mud, their shirts torn, their hands callused.

They looked like Volga boatmen. But instead of boats full of cargo, they hauled the great weight of their misfortune, harnessed to the cart of misery.

And then Papa began to drink.

Oh! Volga, Volga, how wide are your banks. . . .

Chapter 5

I don't know how, nor from where, Papa managed to get the money for the trip. I only know that on a cold winter night, we arrived in Porto Alegre, the state's capital and largest city.

After embracing their friends and relatives, the other passengers, who had come on the same train, were leaving the station area. Only our family remained on the deserted platform. We didn't know anyone and no one knew us.

A railway company employee came over to tell us something.

"Me no understand Brazilian," stammered Papa, completing his thought with gestures.

The official, with a discrete smile, explained to us with more gestures that it was time to shut the station's doors.

We hastily grabbed our bags and exited the station, stopping, undecided, on the sidewalk, not knowing which way to go.

Right away runners approached us offering various services. Papa said no with a shake of his head, looking stunned at the very busy rua Voluntarios da Patria.

Streetcars passed full of people. Automobiles rapidly sped by each other, honking impatiently. Boys ran by hawking the evening newspapers. Men and women, some in pairs, walked hurriedly on the sidewalk with a somber air, preoccupied, swelling the immense human wave that came and went in an uneven and accelerated rhythm.

Forlorn and abandoned, we were saved by a Jewish cart man, who after a short conversation took us to his house, where he generously offered us his modest hospitality.

This merciful man still lives in Porto Alegre. He is, however, almost blind. Because he saw the sufferings of others, God, who is infinitely good, almost took away his sight. . . .

Without money and without a profession, with a large family and in wholly foreign surroundings, only one way to enter this new life remained for Papa—the same way he exited the last, through the gateway of commerce.

He chose the profession of fishmonger, the only one he could carry out within the conditions in which he found himself. It didn't demand much capital or knowledge of the language.

He bought two baskets and, tying them together with a long strap, went to the market, filled them with fish and returned shouting:

"Fis . . . fis . . . baaases."

Mama, who since early in the day had been impatiently waiting for him, recognized his voice and ran to the window. When she saw him in the distance loaded down with baskets advertising his merchandise in loud cries, she left the window exasperated.

Shortly afterward Papa arrived. He entered happily. He pulled the strap off his neck and put his load down on the floor.

"Well," he said, rubbing his hands and straightening up his body. "Today is won. Tomorrow, God will have to help us again."

Seeing his wife sad and imagining her inner displeasure he justified his actions.

"We are in the New World, woman. And here any occupation is acceptable. Honest work is not dishonorable."

Pulling out a fish, he changed the subject,

"Take this and prepare a good lunch. It's getting late, and I still have some rounds to make to sell the rest."

Grabbing the fish without enthusiasm, Mama muttered sighing:

"How nice, what a nice exchange you made. You left the store in Russia to become a fishmonger in Brazil."

Papa didn't respond. He bent down, put the strap around his neck, lifted up the baskets and, casting Mama a reproachful look, he left.

His wife's plaint had hurt him, deeply. He wasn't to blame for the situation they had landed in. He had made the change with the best of intentions. Choosing agriculture, he had thought to give his sons a good future. He couldn't live by exploiting others. His conscience rebelled. He wanted a productive life.

He brushed away the thoughts that were saddening him with his breadwinner's litany,

"Fis . . . fis . . . ."

And every day, at almost the same time, he filled the streets of that neighborhood with the same refrain:

"Fis . . . fis . . . ."

At the end of the first month of work, he rented a house on rua Castro Alves where much of the city's life played out. We moved at night. I think it was to hide our dire poverty.

As fish was only sold in the mornings, Papa used the afternoons to sell fruit. And as soon as he had enough money for two more baskets, Solon and Luiz began to help him selling oranges and bananas.

After a few weeks, Solon got a job selling sweets for a German widow. At night he would wash the dishes for her.

Luiz and Papa worked with enthusiasm committed to the realization of a small dream, to acquire, as soon as possible, a cart and a horse.

Our life flowed along, like that, happy and hopeful. We earned enough to support our family, and we even managed to save some. But conventional wisdom doesn't fail—a poor man's happiness is short-lived. And that's what happened. I fell ill, stricken with a high fever.

At first, my parents thought it was nothing to worry about. But seeing that I grew worse, they decided to take me to *Santa Casa de Misericordia*.

I still have a clear mental image of that Monday morning when I was brought to the hospital.

Wrapped around Papa's neck with my eyes half closed, my heavy head collapsed on his right shoulder, and my body burning up with fever, I was letting myself be carried along the rua da Independencia.

The sun-bathed houses seemed to smile happily behind the white window curtains that the morning breeze opened partway, showing the comfortable interiors of these wealthy residences.

The trees, leaning over the railed walls, festively swayed their gentle fronds as if they were blessing life itself . . . .

I looked with envy at the cheerful bands of clean and well-fed children carrying books under their arms or book packs on their backs going happily to school. As I went by they looked directly at me. Some with pity. Others with ridicule, sticking out their tongues, laughing and making faces. But, even so, I didn't take my eyes off of that beautiful, youthful scene. I envied their happy and worry-free life. And, as someone who imagines the impossible, I thought of the immense pleasure I would have the day that I too, like them, could go to school.

At the hospital, after waiting some time, our turn came. After the examination, the doctor brought us to a man with dark glasses that was seated in the waiting room on a small platform writing in a big book. The doctor said something to him and went back to the examination room.

This clerk with his dark glasses and an expressionless evil looking face posed several questions to Papa, taking note of the answers that an informal interpreter was transmitting. Once he finished the registration questions, the clerk left the table and, making a sign for us to follow him, opened a big wide door that led to the hospital's courtyard, dressed with plants and flowers. From there he brought us into a vast room full of the sick where a nun came to see us. After exchanging a few words with the nurse, she withdrew.

It was an enormous rectangular room, completely whitewashed and with many windows. Along the walls, rows of white hospital beds were stretched out, all alike, and all occupied by adults.

They were dressed in wide cotton shirts that fell over sturdy blue pants. A few, seated on the edge of their beds, conversed with their fellow patients. Others slept, breathing with difficulty. Some were just lying there, moaning.

Right in the middle of the ward, there was a long table for meals. At the head of the table, a large crucifix hung from a tall wooden column.

Realizing that Papa didn't understand what she was saying to him in Portuguese, the sister informed him in German that I had typhoid fever and had to remain in the hospital. He could only see me on the days when visits to the third-class wards were permitted.

Papa grew pale. He couldn't hide how much the seriousness of my illness affected him. He clutched me tightly, kissed me, and left.

The nun took me to a corner of the room where she put up a folding screen and took off my clothes. Then she dressed me in a hospital gown and some short pants that were suspended from the shoulders by strips of cloth. She wrapped up my clothes. She numbered the package and gave it to another nun. She ordered that a little bed be set up for me beside the crucifix. The next day they cut my hair and gave me a hot bath.

I thought of the suffering of my family, who could only see me the following Thursday without knowing if they would find me alive or dead. Except on days set by regulations, visits were rigorously prohibited. In vain Papa did try to see me. They didn't let him in. Hoping that I would appear by chance, he sat down dismayed on a park bench in front of the hospital and stayed there for many hours, with his eyes fixed on a window, which he supposed belonged to my ward. Then he went back into the hospital. And he only left when they informed him that I was getting better.

I stayed in the hospital for more than a month.

Entering convalescence, I was overtaken by an incredible and voracious appetite. No amount of food could satisfy me. That's why I proposed the exchange of chocolate for toasted bread to a boy who served as a nurse's aide in the ward. He agreed and immediately we made the first trade. That night, when everyone seemed to be asleep, I started to gnaw on the bread.

One day I awoke with a fever. Trying to determine the cause and following up on a report from another patient who had denounced us, the nurse discovered that I had stuffed myself with bread obtained clandestinely from the aide.

Proceeding to a search of my bed, the proof of the accusation was found under the pillow.

The aide was punished, and I was forbidden from that day forward to receive either chocolate or toasted bread.

Something else I wasn't able to forget occurred one intensely hot afternoon.

The sun was burning away like a glowing ember in a cloudless sky. There wasn't the slightest breeze. The windows in the ward were all wide open, and even so, the atmosphere in the hospital was suffocating.

The patients were agitated and restless as they fanned themselves.

On the streets where there was scarcely anyone at that sun-drenched hour, the silence was almost complete.

To breath a bit better I leaned out of one of the ward's windows.

Just then I heard a voice, sad like a lament, proclaiming:

"Over here . . . sweets . . . Over here . . . candies . . . "

That voice was not unfamiliar.

I felt a tightening in my heart, and I looked down.

Seated on one of the stone steps of the hospital, a boy was scaring off the flies that were reaching out for his tray of sweets with a piece of cardboard as he sang out in a low voice:

"Over here sweets, over here candies,"

I recognized him right away.

"Solon," I shouted

He lifted his head, looking for me.

It was my brother.

Our eyes met and, filled with the same emotion, we remained speechless for a few moments. Then I smiled sadly. And he did the same. I was so sad for him, seeing him like a ragamuffin selling sweets. And he was so sad for me, seeing me sick in the hospital.

I felt my eyes fill with tears and I couldn't hold them back. I abruptly left the window. I lay down on the bed and smothered my tears in the pillow while every now and then the dying echo of my brother's voice was heard, like a veiled moan, in the sad silence of the ward.

"Over here sweets. . . . Over here candies. . . . "

Chapter 6

The day they let me go from the hospital I jumped for joy.

In spite of being extremely weak and painfully thin, I stomped on the sidewalk cobblestones. The resonance of my own steps filled me with indescribable pleasure. I walked along smiling. Happy. I felt like a victor who had conquered death.

Accustomed to the hospital's dim light, I couldn't stand the blazing sun. I was dazzled. Dizzy. The city's dynamic rumble stunned my ears. They had grown used to the long and painful silences of the wards. Even so, I walked firmly, filled with an inner happiness, breathing deeply, gulping down my new life to clear my lungs of the hospital's foul atmosphere that was saturated with heavy medicinal smells. Once again, I felt the sun's warm, loving touch as it dissolved, filling my soul with warm light-filled kisses.

It was the emotion of a prisoner abruptly restored to freedom after a long incarceration.

I was overcome by a sensation of rebirth. Life had new charms for me. My body felt lighter. The air softer. The light purer. The shade cooler. Humanity kinder. I had a violent urge to embrace and kiss everyone, to shout, loudly, that life is beautiful. And that life is worth living.

During my absence, the family had moved to a major street, rua Esperanca, in the "Colonia Africana" neighborhood where I made my first childhood friendships, where I flew my first kite, where I played with my first spinning top, and where I received the first slaps for the crime of being a descendent of poor Jews.

I remember it very well. It was during my convalescence, days after leaving the hospital.

One afternoon, I was sitting on a rise near our house, watching a few kids playing in an empty lot across the street. I could only enjoy from afar that childhood display of health and glee because my weakened state would not yet permit me to participate in such games.

Suddenly I see a sour-faced boy standing in front of me asking haughtily for my name. I gave it to him.

"You're a Jew, aren't you?"

I confirmed the fact with a nod of my head.

And in answer, he dealt me two violent slaps on my face and continued calmly on his way.

I felt dizzy, stunned by that stupid, unexpected, and unjust aggression.

I couldn't understand how someone could hit his fellow man, without any reason, just for the simple pleasure of seeing him suffer. And I burst out crying, loudly.

Hearing me cry, my mother came running to see what was happening. Between great sobs, I told her what had occurred.

She wanted to hit the boy. But he had already disappeared.

"What can we do, my son?" she said, resignedly, wiping away my tears, "It is our destiny. . . . "

More than physical pain, I felt the pain of moral suffering. The injustice of the attack remained acutely engraved.

When I had returned home from the hospital, I had been received with great displays of joy.

Accustomed to my sullen family, I wished, later on, to fall ill again so that I could bring them once more such contentment. So much so, that I ardently desired to remain in a perpetual state of convalescence so that they would always be happy.

Unfortunately, I was restored to health. And they recovered their habitual sadness.

Solon was still employed at the German widow's house. Luiz, however, had been promoted, becoming a prominent industrialist. He was selling ice cream from a two-wheeled handcart.

Manufactured at home, the ice cream was simply worthless. As a rule, it lacked sugar or had too much salt. It was enough to try it only one time to never buy it again. Even the children made fun of my brother:

"Look at the kid with salty ice cream."

And shouted in chorus:

"Sal-tee i-ce cre-am

Sal–tee i-ce cre-am. . . . "

Luiz pushed the cart, blowing on a metal horn, carried on a shoulder strap over a white apron, under the harsh burning sun that on days of intense heat transformed the city into an enormous furnace. At every corner he stopped, blowing the horn. And in his instrument's voice, there was a great lament, an enormous human protest against a world that lets children sacrifice their childhood to the conquest of a meager piece of bread.

More and more Papa gave himself up to drink.

He didn't work any longer on foot. He had bought a wagon and a horse.

He left the fruit trade to dedicate himself, exclusively, to fish. He now had a small clientele, more or less steady, the majority landsmen, fellow Jews.

Fridays were his big day when he usually made the most sales of the week. Because the Jews, in general, those of the old generation, don't cook on Saturdays, their day of rest. So, they prepare the food for Saturday on the day before, and stuffed fish is an almost indispensable dish.

The day of rest begins Fridays at sunset.

At that moment, when the evening star appears, the dinner, as well as the following day's lunch, is ready. The house is straightened, clean, joyful.

The wife extends the best cloth over the table and puts down a challah, braided wheat bread, made especially for this ceremony. When there is no challah, she serves ordinary bread. She covers the bread with a napkin and places the polished candlesticks with new candles on the side. She puts a scarf on her head. She lights the candles. She covers her face with her hands. She concentrates for a few moments. And, then, joining her palms in front of the candlesticks, she begins to recite the blessing for the candles, praying softly.

Once the prayer is finished, all work is suspended until the same time on the following day.

At that twilight hour, the poorest tables acquire the sacred appearance of modest altars. And the fragrant host of fresh bread, the slow burning of the blessed candles, and the mysticism of nightfall transform the poorest homes into humble temples, where can be found throbbing, full of life, the religious faith of the Jew who holds up his soul to the Creator and implores divine mercy for his endless misfortunes . . . .

Chapter 7

After I regained my health, I was enrolled with Daniel in a *cheder* that was run in an old building near our house, in an enormous room with entirely bare walls, without maps and without blackboards.

The *cheder* is the Jewish primary school where children are taught to read and write in Yiddish and Hebrew and translate the Bible from Hebrew to Yiddish, the language commonly spoken among Jews. Only a minority, represented by the priests and some poets and writers, which constitute the elite of Jewish intellectuals, write and speak in Hebrew, a language that I understand has been officially adopted in Palestine.

Jews today have fully recast education, structuring learning according to the most advanced methods of modern pedagogy. But in my time the lamentable antiquated system prevailed.

The director of the school usually reflected the ridiculous and traditional image of an old Jew with a filthy Talmudic beard. With long and dirty fingernails. With an over-sized silky black alpaca jacket, a derby hat, and an umbrella.

He sat in the classroom at the head of a long table. Next to him lay a cane or switch, a classical symbol of authority. On each side of the table, on long benches, sat the students.

Designated by the teacher, one of the students began the reading and the translation of the Bible. The others accompanied the lesson in silence. The following section was handled by the second student. Then the duty passed to the third. And like this, the reading continued, successively until the last student, always in order.

However, there were times, and they weren't so rare when students were randomly called on to read their portion. From the first student on a bench, the call went to the last on the opposite bench. And if that one, taken by surprise, weren't able to immediately pick up the thread of the readings, he would be punished, without mercy. The switch would whiz through the stern atmosphere of the classroom, cracking on the back of the distracted one. The victim would cringe in pain. If he cried, he would catch even more. He couldn't protest. He had to suffer in silence. Only the children of more well-off families were spared. The old man usually turned a blind eye to the more severe wrongdoings that they committed. And when, exceptionally, he felt obliged to punish them, he gave them such soft slaps that they had the tenderness of true caresses.

It is in school that class distinctions are revealed.

With this barbaric method, condemned by Jewish literature in one of its most vigorous and moving novels, Jewish educators tried to inculcate in students the love of learning.

The old man followed the tradition of shut but attentive eyes. When he thought a student was distracted, he ordered him calmly,

"Go ahead, Jose."

Jose, whose thoughts were centered on much more interesting things than the Bible, turned red, trembling, unsuccessfully trying to find the point where his classmate had suspended the reading. Per the teacher's orders, his classmates couldn't help him without being branded accomplices.

There was a nervous silence, followed by anxious expectations. The cane whirred through the air falling forcefully on the back of the victim, who writhed in pain and began to sob quietly, repressing his tears.

I almost believe that the "rebbe" secretly enjoyed the corporal punishments. It seems to me that he found a certain pleasure in them, the pleasure of a moral sadist.

One time we revolted against these untempered punishments. We made the switch disappear.

Contrary to what happens among adults, no one denounced the leader of the plan. We all caught the bony hand of our executioner. Yet the switch did not reappear.

But even so, the pernicious consequences of that brutal system of instruction remained deeply and indelibly engraved.

Chapter 8

Before the end of the school year, I began to work with Daniel in a Jewish butcher shop.

We made home deliveries.

The Jewish faith, as was previously explained, only permits the consumption of meat slaughtered by one of the community's priests, the *shochet,* who, except on Saturdays, goes daily to the public slaughterhouse to sacrifice the needed cattle.

It is a sacrilege to eat "treif," non-kosher food. That's why every Jewish community has at least one butcher of its own.

Although, today, this and other religious precepts are only observed by some old orthodox Jews. Younger people have abandoned them, only respecting those parts of the ancestral beliefs that are not incompatible with modern civilization and culture. These, as a rule, are simple prescriptions for hygiene and the maintenance of corporal and mental health.

Driven by this new way of life, young Jews have long since broken the chains that enslaved them to an age-old and antiquated tradition, integrating slowly into the world around them and adopting its habits, practices, and customs. And, day-by-day, they are gradually expanding the boundaries of their moral and intellectual emancipation. But their complete liberation can only be attained when they assimilate with other races, mixing their blood with the blood of other peoples so that from this successive crossbreeding, from this progressive welding, can arise a happier future for poor humanity and generations free from unjust hatreds and absurd prejudices stemming from the concept of racial aristocracy—sinisterly created in the land of Goethe. Because, made of the same clay, all the peoples and races that cover the face of the earth are just different members of the great one and only human family.

It is true that believers in assimilation recently saw their convictions severely shaken by the barbarous behavior of Hitler's Germany that persecuted and tortured descendants of Jews who had long ago adopted German ways and completely divorced themselves from their Semitic ancestors.

Notwithstanding, we can conclude, based on an examination and analysis of the true motives behind the inhuman and unspeakable persecutions of the Nazis, that they are the same motives that have always propelled all anti-Semitic movements, and that the painful German phenomenon does not represent the generalized feeling of the German people. Rather, it solely represents the feelings of one man, with immeasurable political ambitions, and the feelings of the fanatics that sustain him in power.[1]

We got up way before daybreak. And, without breakfast, incased in Papa's old jackets that fell over our knees, we left for the butcher shop.

On the street, it was still night. The stars sparkled in the tranquil sky. And the city slept, peacefully, wrapped in a great silence that sometimes at our passing the barking of dogs disturbed.

In nearby puddles, frogs croaked.

Vegetable sellers seated on the rims of their carts went slowly to the market, crushing the silence of the night with the rolling of their vehicles on the uneven stones of the streets.

When we arrived at the butcher's, we found the meat, already properly weighed and rolled up in old newspapers, with the name and address of each customer written in pencil, in Yiddish.

The route allotments completed, we grabbed our straw hampers and left to deliver the orders to the customers.

On winter mornings, the work was painful.

The cold from the stones of the sidewalk penetrated our bare feet like needles. We walked hunched over, freezing, protecting ourselves from the insanely hissing wind that whipped our icy and stiffened bodies.

As we delivered our parcels, the weight diminished, and our relief expanded.

Harsh complaints directed to our boss followed us everywhere. Generally, the customers weren't pleased with the meat that had been chosen for them. They always found some reason to grumble. Either the meat was too fatty or too lean. Extremely rare were the times when they were satisfied.

The old women turned over everything in the hamper, rifling through the parcels and undoing many of them, finishing by sending the butcher to hell or condemning him to contorted and lonely nighttime pleasures. Meanwhile, the butcher made prodigious calculations trying to satisfy everyone, something he hardly ever achieved.

After some months, I left the butcher shop and went to work in a small grocery store belonging to my former teacher from Quatro Irmãos who, after we came to Porto Alegre, also abandoned the colony, exchanging the teacher's platform for a shopkeeper's counter.

He was about thirty years old, tall, elegant, with lively blue eyes, a short blondish mustache, and a closely shaved face. He walked, spoke, and ate with extreme rapidity.

He had been a teacher in the schools of our district. And he had, among other defects, a lamentable weakness for women. He didn't even respect his own students. He used to fondle them lasciviously while he helped them individually with their lessons as they stood in front of his desk. To better satisfy his lewd desires, he took the precaution of placing his platform and his desk behind the students' benches, keeping an eye on them from their backs. Even so, we peeked at him through the angle formed by our upper and forearms. But we never caught him in the act.

But one time, while the teacher was explaining the lesson, a girl, the prettiest in our class, feeling below her skirt his lustful fingers groping her, gave him right in the middle of the classroom a thunderous slap on his face, thoroughly humiliating him.

The scandal was immediately broadcast and taken by the parents to the administration and, for some time, the teacher's situation became precarious. However, he kept his position. And as a consequence, there was a noted decrease in feminine attendance.

My job at this small shop consisted of waiting on customers at the counter and delivering purchases to their homes.

I don't remember anymore how long I remained at that job. I only know that I worked from the first hours of the morning to late at night.

In the mornings, I lit the fire. I opened and swept the store. I made coffee for the family. I prepared the bottle for the boss' little girl. And I also executed other tasks that had nothing to do with my job.

One night, when I was taking a can of kerosene in a handcart to a customer's house, I accidentally met up with Papa, near the Garibaldi cinema. He asked me if I had had dinner. I said no.

"Not yet?" he exclaimed indignantly. "And that scoundrel of your boss dares to make you work until these hours? Let go of that can! I didn't bring up my sons to be slaves."

I obeyed. He took the can of kerosene to the customer, himself. I followed him in silence, on the sidewalk. On the way back, he sent me home saying that he was going to settle accounts with my employer.

The next day Papa told me that he had taken me out of that job. Deep down, I rejoiced, overtaken by a delicious sense of freedom.

Sometime later Papa told me,

"I arranged a place for you in a pharmacy. It is clean and light work. It is a place with a future. You can still become somebody one day."

I received the news with great satisfaction. I imagined myself in a white apron, preparing medicines.

I shared this news with my friends who began to render me special consideration.

Papa had made for me a lightweight brown suit of clothes with long pants. The shirt's closed collar suited me well. He bought me new shoes. And he advised me that the following Monday I would present myself to my new employer.

On the appointed day, I woke up early, impatient to go. And Papa took me to the pharmacy.

The pharmacy was in a big two-story building, recently built. On the top floor lived the boss' family. On the ground floor was the pharmacy.

During the first days, my only duty was to carry the rubble that the masons had left in various apartments in the building to a vacant lot across the street. Once this was done, I started to work in the store.

I began by washing the glass containers, with soap and sand, in a large washtub behind the building. After cleaning them, I stacked them on the shelves in a room next to the compounding lab. I was also tasked with washing the equipment used to handle the medicines.

Sometimes I delivered medicines to the customers' homes. And it was during the exercise of this duty that on one occasion I almost involuntarily killed a man.

It happened this way.

The owner of the pharmacy was Jewish. But he didn't like to speak Yiddish. In spite of knowing that I understood very little Portuguese, he wouldn't make an exception. He only spoke in Portuguese.

One time he told me to deliver two bottles of medicine that contained different liquids, explaining,

"From the smaller one, the patient should take one teaspoon every two hours. And he should drink the larger bottle all at once."

"Yes, sir," I responded, even though I didn't know the difference between the words *smaller* and *larger*. I was too embarrassed to ask him to clarify in Yiddish, so I just left.

In the house of the patient, who was Jewish, I assumed the air of importance of a doctor and recommended to the person who came to speak to me precisely the opposite of what I had been told, ordering the patient to drink the smaller bottle all at once and to take the medicine in the larger one in small doses.

I don't know why, but at my return, my employer decided to inquire in Yiddish how I had fulfilled my mission.

"I said take the medicine in the small bottle all at once and the medicine in the large one by teaspoons every two hours."

The man grew pale, exclaiming furiously,

"*Burro*, you poisoned the patient."

In a panic, he called for his wife and ran out without his hat.

I trembled. The notion of having caused the death of a man was destroying me. I felt crushed by tragic images. Suicidal thoughts were assaulting me. I was overwrought, my torment greatly oppressing my heart.

Half an hour later, which seemed to me half a century, my employer returned. From the compounding room where I fretfully waited for him, I could hear him say to his wife,

"Happily, I arrived in time. The poor devil is safe."

And he added,

"We can't have any confidence in our employees. They're imbeciles."

She came to my defense,

"The boy is not at fault. You should have given him the instructions in Yiddish. You know very well that he only recently came from Russia and he still doesn't know the language of this new land very well."

He didn't say anything. But, from that day forth, he communicated with me in the language of the Jews.

When I knew that the patient was saved, I breathed again, relieved. I had the feeling of being reborn. I regained my spirit, and I threw myself into my work with great enthusiasm.

To compensate for the scare, the next day brought me a tiny and unexpected joy that I fondly enshrined in the very bottom of my heart.

I was washing the glassware in the courtyard, thinking about the mistake of the night before.

It was afternoon, and it was very warm. The water in the washtub was scalding. The sand I was putting in the bottles was so hot that it seemed to be made of embers. Suddenly, I heard someone call me. I looked up and saw my boss' daughter, signaling from the upper floor for me to come up.

Her name was Rita. She was an only child. More or less my age. . . .

I cleaned my hands. I took off the apron. And with my heart beating fast, I went up the stairs.

"It is very hot outside," she said to me, smiling. "Come rest in here a little."

Perceiving my natural embarrassment, she tried to put me at ease.

"Don't be afraid. My parents aren't home. They went to the docks to say goodbye to a friend who is leaving today for Rio. Come in."

I obeyed, passing into a richly furnished room.

The balcony windows were open. From behind the blinds, a soft light filtered through. The rugs, furniture, and crystal gave off a vivid sensation of well-being. Everything exuded order, peace, and comfort.

On a table covered with a pure white cloth, there was a teapot, two cups, and cookies.

"Please, won't you sit down," asked the girl in a gentle voice, pointing to a chair.

Feeling very shy, I sat down. I looked around at everything, full of admiration.

I had never seen the inside of a wealthy person's house.

Nothing there called to mind the misery of my world. This was a world different from the world I knew. A better world made of fine things for fine people. It was a world created on a higher plane of life, a plane altogether unknown to me.

I contemplated, with naïve pride, the city that extended itself at my feet.

I didn't know yet that in many lowly homes lived high ideals and that in many high placed homes, only lowly feelings could be found.

"Would you accept a cup of tea?"

I answered yes.

She served me the tea, looking at me with kindness and speaking to me with tenderness.

I listened to her in silence, truly moved. It was the first time that a stranger had spoken to me with affection. I wanted her to feel my enormous gratitude for the interest and friendship she was showing me, so I stood up, but, "thank you, thank you very much," was all I managed to utter. And I went down to the courtyard.

I put on the apron, and with sadness, I began again my interrupted task.

The time spent with Rita, upstairs, felt like a dream. I stood there, lost in my thoughts, remembering. And I saw her image in the dirty water of the washtub, smiling, holding out to me a cup of tea. I recalled the room, the furniture, the crystal, and the city seen from above.

It was the second time in my poor boy existence that I contemplated life from an upper story. The first time, however, was from the windows of *Santa Casa* . . . .

Chapter 9

While I worked at the pharmacy, Luiz and Solon abandoned ice cream and sweets, dedicating themselves to peddling odds and ends, a trade practiced by many Jewish immigrants at that time, as it didn't demand much capital or knowledge of the language.

They left the house each morning with a pile of small boxes containing socks, ties, and bars of soap in one hand and in the other, a basket full of knickknacks. Like children of the streets, they covered the city on foot throughout the day, knocking on doors from one to the next and shouting into houses through open doors or windows,

"Socks, soap, fine tooth combs. . . . "

They weren't always well received. At times, but only rarely, doors were closed violently in their faces, or they were shooed away like dogs,

"Get out of here!"

They received these offenses without a word. In spite of the indignation, they were resigned.

It is the lot of a poor Jew to be humiliated, despised, scorned, mistreated, persecuted, and decimated as in the Russian pogroms—massive massacres of Jews. For the simple act of having given to humanity a Jesus Christ, many martyrs, saints, and heroes, and apostles of science, art, and faith, and for the heinous crime of having left to the world an invaluable moral and cultural heritage that fills the human species with just pride, the miserable Jew, since being expulsed from his home, many centuries ago, drags across the earth the weight of his disgrace, having to implore humanity to give him a place in the sun and the basic right to life because the kingdom of truth and justice has not yet dawned for all.

And like this, knocking door to door, all day long, they filled the streets with the old and well-known refrain that even today a legion of poor Jews sings through the quarters of many cities so as not to cry,

"Sooocks . . . sooocks . . . sooocks."

Life at home was dragging along full of troubles and hardships.

No merciful ray of light came to cheer up our sad and somber existence. Our own pains and sorrows constantly embittered each of us. Rare, very rare were the moments of happiness that we reaped from our childhood.

The windows and doors remained almost always closed so as not to show the world the intimate dramas that unfolded inside. And we endured with stoic resignation, in anguished silence, the humiliation of our misfortune that during many years made us shed bitter tears of quiet desperation.

Besides poverty, destiny gave us a cross too heavy to bear, the cross of shame.

My father drank, which caused us intense suffering.

Almost daily he came home intoxicated, filling the house with sadness and the smell of *cachaca.*

Mother, prematurely aged, cried constantly, bemoaning the lot life had given her and bewailing the fate of her children.

With pleas and threats, she spent her days asking Papa to give up his damned vice. But either he didn't answer, or he claimed that it was useless for her to insist, that nothing could be done, that it was beyond his control and therein began arguments, disputes, and painful scenes that usually ended in wailing tears.

When, at night, we returned from work and didn't find him in the house, it was certain that he would come home drunk. We had dinner in silence, foreseeing what was coming. A cloud of boundless despair descended over us all, filling us with worry. And, miserably distressed, we awaited the unfolding of the daily drama. Finally, Papa arrived. He came in staggering, exhaling a strong smell of spirits.

The silence grew, portending the imminence of the storm. It didn't wait long to break out, with a roar.

Mama immediately demanded to know,

"Why did you come home so late?"

He didn't answer.

"Where have you been until now?" she insisted, raising her voice.

He remained silent.

"Why don't you speak?" she hollered, frantic from this stubborn silence. "You think this won't end one day? You are mistaken . . . very mistaken. . . . You will see. . . . It will end! I am fed up with you and this miserable life. . . . I can't put up any longer with this drawn-out torment. I am tired of suffering. I am going to leave you with your damned vice. Then you can drink all you want. I'll work as a servant, wherever I can, and I will learn how to honestly earn my bread. The heaviest work would be much lighter than this wretched life. At least I will have peace and tranquility, living without humiliations . . . at the side of my children. Poor children that bear so much. . . . Because of them, I have put up with you until now, you spineless creature. They were small . . . I had to resign myself. . . . Now, thank God, they are grown. . . . They can help me . . . they won't abandon their poor, unhappy mother."

"Go see if the horse has food and water," Papa ordered me as if he had not paid any attention to his wife's threats.

"Don't go," my mother countermanded. "If he loves his horse more than his sons, let him go himself." Becoming more and more irritated she pressed ahead, barely containing the rage that was fermenting in her heart,

"What are you thinking? Why are you silent? Until when do you plan to keep mortifying us?"

And, changing her voice to a begging tone,

"For the love of God, have some compassion for your family, for your disgraced family. Have mercy, have pity on your poor sons."

Papa lifted his head and stared at Mother with an abstract, distant look. Then with a tender voice, he asked her,

"Please, leave me alone. Leave me alone . . . I'm hungry."

"Leave you alone, why?" Mother exploded exasperated. And with an ironic inflection in her words,

"Yes . . . , the day won't be long before I will leave you. . . . But it will be forever . . . do you hear? Forever. . . . You bandit, you miserable man, you drunk!"

Papa didn't answer. He drew back, cowering.

He knew his wife very well. He knew that she would be incapable of carrying out the threat, which had been reiterated innumerable times. He knew that the next day they would reconcile, and she would forgive him everything, as she had always done.

In a moment of extreme despair, not able to contain the wave of outrage that filled her chest, Mother slapped him across the face, exclaiming,

"Take that one, you drunk. . . . "

And then her nerves utterly collapsed.

We brought her to the bedroom where she threw herself on the bed, shaken by convulsive crying.

This scene no longer shocked us. We were used to it. We felt ashamed. The pain of the slap burned on our own cheeks.

No one dared speak. A dreary and heavy silence invaded the house becoming almost funeral in the smoldering lamplight.

From the bedroom, Mother's choked sobs cut through our hearts. And we too began to cry until, vanquished by slumber and exhaustion, we slept.

The next day, feeling very low, we returned to work. We couldn't forget the scene from the night before. We looked with envy on the happiness of the children that didn't know the miseries of alcohol and that didn't have to hide from the eyes of the world the shame of having a drunken father.

And like this, for many long years, in the shadow of our misery, we played out this anonymous drama of our destiny, while enduring in silence the irreparable pain of our misfortune.

As I grew up, however, experience revealed to me other dramas portrayed daily on the great stage of life, anonymous like ours, but much more heart wrenching and painful.

Chapter 10

Hoping to change our luck, we moved, going to live on rua Jose do Patrocinio, the old rua Concordia, where my parents opened a little modest fruit store.

On the eve of the move, I left the pharmacy.

Papa's hopes and my naïve dream were totally thwarted. The same ignorance that had accompanied me when I entered the pharmacy followed me out the door.

In truth, now I was allowed, from time to time, to sell cocoa butter at the counter. But I still continued to wash dirty bottles and greasy devices.

A few days before leaving this job, in recompense for the months of unpaid service that I had given him, my boss, out of the goodness of his heart, in a magnanimous gesture, with evident interest in my future, promoted me, entrusting me with a high level, delicate, and extremely important duty—filling small cans with Vaseline.

For sure, to become a full-fledged pharmacist, I lacked very little. . . .

I then began to practice another profession. Not as clean but much more profitable—poultry sales.

Barefoot, pants attached to my waist by a thick cord and falling just below my knees, I carried the hens by their legs, their heads hanging down, as I set out with Daniel, my brother and partner in this and other businesses, to shout through the streets of our neighborhood, full of youngsters,

"Hear, hear, faaaaat hens. . . . Hear, hear, faaaaat chicken."

And the echo repeated in the distance,

" . . . aaaaaat . . . "

This work was entertaining. It had the flavor of an adventure. Daniel strived to perfect his chant, imprinting his voice with a certain melody.

"Psst . . . psst . . . , boys!"

We turned around pleased, already tasting the pleasure of a realized sale. And the dialogue started.

"Are these chicken fat?"

"Yes, they are, my dame," trying to speak elegantly in our new language but not quite making it.

"Let me see."

The customer chose two birds. She held them up in the air one in each hand, verifying the difference in weight. Then, she examined them, patting them. She blew on the feathers that covered the breast and those that were under the tail. Finally, keeping the best one, she inquired,

"How much do you want for this chicken?"

"Fifteen hundred."

"It's very expensive. Not for me."

"It's not eee pensive, mam. Take it."

"For that price, no. Even the other day much prettier chickens than these were selling for fifteen hundred."

"Ok, just so I don't have to take it home you can have it for fourteen hundred."

The money in our pockets, we returned to hawking our wares with renewed enthusiasm. The neighborhood boys began to mock us, shouting,

"Eh, Jews!"

We pretended not to hear. However, they insisted,

"Jews . . . Hey, we're talking to you, Jews. . . . "

Indignant from our indifference, they jeered at us, insulting us with offensive words. Then, they went from insults to physical aggression, throwing stones at us.

Later, by accident, I found the principal source of this rancor against the Jews. It was in some schools, run by clerics. Corrupting their higher mission, certain Fathers tried to instill this racial hatred in the virgin and impressionable minds of children. To do this, they invented the most absurd stories. In the school's chapel, as a student in one of these institutions, I had the opportunity to hear bald-headed tales, incredible things that instead of love for others, as preached by Christ, transmitted the seed of hate, cultivated by the clerical imagination.

Now as I stretch my memory to look back at the world of my childhood, with the inexperienced eyes of that small chicken peddler that I was, I recognize that back then I faced life gripped by a precocious and intuitive resignation, which allowed me to be led by the invisible hand of destiny without reluctance or desire.

I wasn't moved by any ambition. But I felt capable of the greatest sacrifices to lessen the pain of those who suffer without solace. Particularly those close to me. Their situation pierced me straight through. Mother's tears and the tears of my brothers made me suffer horribly. The problems that Papa caused them, with his drinking, filled me with indignation.

I tortured my juvenile soul to discover what led him to drink. An internal voice told me that he didn't give himself up to drink just for pleasure. That he drank for compelling reasons that I still ignored. And I let myself be persuaded by this voice and thought, "really Papa is a good man." He has a very sensitive heart. Surely, he turns to alcohol because it pains him to see his family reduced to their deplorable situation. And I attributed his chronic sadness to his material wretchedness, his inability to assure us a better life.

In the face of these and other reflections, I silently revolted against the world in which all the creatures that suffer and grit their teeth, without a sound, voiceless, like Papa in his misfortune, appeared to my boy's eyes as simple victims, that drank only to drown their misery in alcohol. They drank for seeing their wives without comfort and their children without education.

A vague and almost instinctive sense of justice made me truly feel, for the first time, the hardships caused by human injustices whose origin and breadth escaped my juvenile perceptions.

That's why, examining my heart, I don't find any nostalgia for the past.

When I opened my eyes of understanding to the world, I saw only misery and sadness, with their funeral procession of tears and sighs, complaints and laments.

During the years when children make the sweetest memories, I received jeers and stones. Never even crumbs of affection or the comfort of an embrace, except for the one I received on the farm from my mother the day I lost my first brother.

For as much as I step back in time, trying to understand myself, I don't find in my affective memory the remembrance of any other one.

Never did I have the delight of hearing in our house one of those pretty stories of princes and fairies, of dwarfs and giants, of good and evil genies. The stories I heard were about fish, hens, and odds and ends. And of boys that hurled stones at us.

Imagination is like fire. It needs fuel. And the fuel I found to nurture mine was dampened by tears. It only burned a little giving off much smoke, making me glimpse the world through a thick black curtain . . . .

That's why in the sanctuary of my memory I only keep one nostalgic image, the image of two elderly people that I knew at that time.

One afternoon, when I was walking alone, selling hens, I passed by a wide iron gate and saw an elderly couple seated in the garden in the shade of a tree, enjoying the cooler air.

I offered them the hens. They signaled to me to enter.

I pushed the gate and went in. They welcomed me graciously. They looked at me kindly. They spoke with tenderness. They asked how old I was. Where I lived. And a number of other questions.

I answered them in a Portuguese turned inside out, mutilating the language.

"So small," they murmured, in admiration. "And already earning a living all by himself."

They bought all the chickens I had. And they told me some things that I could not understand, but I guessed. I felt that they were friendly words.

As it was getting late, I said goodbye and left.

At night, that same day, those two elderly people, going to the cinema, passed by our little store. Seeing me, they stopped. They asked my mother if she would allow me to go with them to the Garibaldi Cinema that was nearby and where they used to go every night.

Very grateful and flattered, Mother let me go. I put on a white sailor shirt with a blue collar, threw on my wooden clogs and went happily with them.

When we entered the cinema, the dry and noisy tic-tac of my little clogs immediately caught the attention of the audience that became annoyed at the clatter they made. But my protectors didn't give any importance to the general surprise. They chose their usual seats and placed me at their side, greeting their acquaintances who didn't take their eyes off of me. And from that day on, whenever Mother consented, they took me to that house of entertainment.

Later on, we moved to another city. But I didn't forget the gesture of that elderly couple that remained imprinted forever. And as I advanced in years, my admiration for them grew, as I remembered the nights when they took me with them to the cinema, this small chicken peddler known to all in those humble outskirts. They didn't consider their social reputations diminished, as they stood up to the silent censure and the comments of their acquaintances. And when, some years later, I was again in Porto Alegre, I went to find them. The small chicken peddler was now a student.

Arriving at the street where they lived, I retraced the places where I once roamed, moved by memories, looking to no avail for the wide iron gate with the old house. It didn't exist anymore. I found, in its place, a modern bungalow.

With my heart trembling, I knocked on the door. I heard steps inside. Right away, a young girl appeared. I asked for the old couple. She responded that she didn't know them. Nor could she give me the least information about them.

I apologized to her and turned back deeply saddened for not having been able to clasp against my heart, in an embrace full of yearning and appreciation, the noble hearts of those two sainted creatures.

Life, after all, is just like that. It rarely shows compassion for our dearest desires.

Chapter 11

Widening our field of activity, Daniel and I started to speculate, buying kerosene cans, empty sacks, and old pieces of lead.

We made a two-wheeled pushcart. And with the profit from the chickens, we began to pursue this new line of business.

One of us pushed the cart through the city streets, while the other followed on the sidewalks, singing out,

"Empty bottles, used lead . . . emppptyyy . . . bottles. . . . "

Buying a bottle here, another there, some sacks or a piece of an old lead pipe a little further down the road, we went along like this, slowly filling our cart. To the bottles that protruded from the body of this small vehicle, we tied metal strands that we had run through the loopholes of empty cans that banged on the roughly laid cobblestones, with a clamor similar to the theatrical tricks used in playhouses and talking movie palaces to imitate thunderstorms.

We sold the product of our purchases to our better-established fellow peddlers who, in general, acquired their merchandise from small time buyers.

We went out each day in the morning, crisscrossing on foot the places furthest from the city's center as the center was already being well covered by our competitors; we chose, as our preferred routes, distant places, hard to reach or infrequently visited areas, still untouched by this kind of business.

At that time, many Jews, both children, and adults, dedicated themselves to this line of work, for the same reasons that brought us to it.

Many times, while we pushed our cart full of bottles, cans and old lead, tired, sweaty, covered with the dust of the streets, there were children playing happily on the sidewalks. We stared at them with certain envy, thinking of our poor joyless childhood.

We were also taken by an enormous desire to play with them. To run, to jump, without worries, perfectly free. But this desire didn't go beyond being a mere dream that life had reserved for children more fortunate than us.

Our intuitive understanding of reality was way beyond our years.

Our childhood was meant for another purpose—to pull out of the world's rubbish the bitter bread of our sad existence. . . .

Chapter 12

Round about the year 19. . . , we moved to Santa Maria, a pretty city surrounded by hills and rolling grassland where a period of relative prosperity and well-being began for us.

Papa rented a building on the main avenue and opened a store selling used clothing and other used items that he spiced up with some new pieces. A mixture of a bric-a-brac shop and a dry goods store.

Some days after our move, I began a relationship with the girl whose extraordinary gracefulness lit the first romantic flame in my boyish heart.

She was the daughter of a German family that lived close to our house. Every afternoon she would come over to play with me in the backyard in the shade of some tall old mulberry trees.

Until then I had not seen so much grace and beauty in a child.

She was fair-haired. And she had a perfect little face, like a doll. Blue eyes, very innocent and very sweet. And fine, delicate skin. She was reminiscent of an enchanted little princess, who had escaped from a book of fairy tales.

I didn't tire of looking at her, of admiring her elegant and slender figure. And the more I observed her, the more beautiful I found her, the more I wanted her, the more I loved her.

Her blond hair swelled my heart with gladness as if her locks were filling it with light, making it vibrate with a strange and profound emotion.

I truly adored her. And the emotions that I experienced, I didn't feel again, never again, neither in my adolescence nor as a grown man.

They are emotions that belong to childhood.

One afternoon, a rainy afternoon, I still remember it well; I was arranging one of the store's windows, wholly absorbed by my task. Just then, I looked outside and saw her, staring at me from the street.

Once the first shock, caused by the surprise, subsided, I signaled to her to enter. I thought her presence at that hour was strange. And I noted that she was somewhat worried.

I asked her what the matter was, as she didn't seem her normal self. Then she confessed with certain embarrassment that she had come to alert me that she couldn't play with me anymore. That her parents, who were Protestants, didn't want our friendship to continue.

"Why?" I inquired right away.

"Because your parents are Jews."

The answer was a blow to my whole being. I was stunned. I felt the blood halt in my veins. I wanted to speak, to show her the injustice of racial prejudice. But my emotions had completely seized my voice.

In silence, I stared at her for quite a while, like someone who beholds a pretty toy that suddenly breaks into pieces.

She sensed the pain that her words had caused me. With sorrow, she squeezed my hand and left.

I leaned my forehead on the glass of the closed door, looking out and thinking of the girl's last words.

The low, somber sky was filling the shut houses and the deserted wet streets with a vast layer of gloom. All around me everything seemed to lament my loss. The sadness expressed increased my own suffering. An enormous feeling of abandonment overcame me, afflicting my heart. And the anguish kept growing, swelling, until it turned into tears. I couldn't contain myself and began to cry as I watched life from behind two clouds of fog, the one that was rising out of my wounded soul and the other that was descending slowly from the steep breasts of the hills.

They were the first, but not the last tears I shed. Afterwards, along the road of life, I let fall many others to soften the stones that tore apart my dearest dreams. But of lovesick tears, those were the only ones. The others were out of pure despair. . . .

I was crestfallen for many days, thinking of the young girl. I fled from the company of my friends, seeking solitude. I didn't feel like doing anything. I was full of pessimistic thoughts. I couldn't resign myself to this doleful separation. I considered myself the most unfortunate of creatures and I thought of suicide.

With time, though, the wound was healing. The romantic crisis that lasted for months ended, leaving deep-set imprints. Then, I was taken with a desire to study, to learn, a desire that arose, perhaps, from the subterranean layers of the unconscious, anxious to discover the causes of prejudice and hatred of the Jews.

Coincident with this intellectual awakening, I met a boy who later became my closest and best friend. For having a big and very generous heart, along with an extremely sensitive soul, he greatly suffered and still suffers as part of this world, where usually the wicked receive the best share of life's offerings.

His father, now deceased, who was best known through the name of his commercial establishment, gained wide popularity throughout the city while alive, thanks to his eccentric and original personality.

He came from England, where he was a peddler of chinaware, to become a farmer in the Philippson colony, situated near the city of Santa Maria.

Not reaping the desired reward from the earth, he left the agricultural tasks in the care of his family and came to the city to find another livelihood. He walked around, observing and sniffing all he saw, with empty pockets and his hands behind his back. He passed by a blacksmith shop with a door on the side leading to a small space for rent. He stopped, scratching his chin, to inspect from the outside this unoccupied cubicle. He confirmed that it was an excellent spot for any type of trade. It was located on the city's most important avenue just where great numbers of arriving passengers brushed by as they poured out of converging trains.

That low dirty door could open up for him a beautiful future, he thought.

Feeling keenly satisfied with his discovery, he thrust his hands into his pockets, exploring them through and through. They were cleaned out. But he wouldn't let himself be discouraged. He began to consider various points. Finally, he made a decision.

He rented that cave the same day. He asked for, and obtained from an acquaintance, a loan of ten thousand reis (roughly thirty US dollars today). With that money, he bought several pairs of old boots, some used hats, suit jackets without pants and pants without jackets. He took his used merchandise to his little rented space. He arranged everything. And, the next day, he put on display at the door one hat, a pair of shoes and a jacket. Then he waited for customers, and it didn't take long for them to gradually begin to appear. With the little bit he sold, he bought a lot more. By the end of the first week, leaning on the wall in front of his establishment, were a washbasin, a table, a bed, and a clothes iron.

Friday, in the late afternoon, he closed his store and walked the twelve miles to Philipson to spend the Sabbath at home with his family.

After a few months, he managed to bring his family to the city. His business was visibly prospering. That cubicle could no longer hold all the merchandise. He rented another one, a larger one, next door. Shortly, this one was also overflowing with beds, stoves and other furniture that he was snapping up at auctions and acquiring from private homes.

Within a few years, the store was well stocked and well established. Santa Maria was now too small to supply it with enough of the type of merchandise it needed. So he went to find supplies in larger urban centers, in Porto Alegre, in São Paulo, in Rio. His commercial contacts grew. His credit did also. He began to buy brand new goods.

When he reached a relatively comfortable economic level, with his family leading a happy life, his wife went insane. He took her to the best specialists in Porto Alegre and Montevideo. He spent a fortune. But it came to naught. After some years of suffering, the poor lady died. The old man's temperament changed in every respect, becoming impossible. His oldest sons soon dispersed. The younger ones left too. Only his daughters remained.

One day he fell ill, gravely ill. Surrounded by his children who had come to help him during his illness, he spent the last days of his life in a hospital.

"The greatest aspiration of my life was to die in my own bed. However, even this was refused to me. . . ," he said before he expired.

My friend was a student in the *Colégio Elementar*. I asked him how I could enter the same school, telling him of my immense desire to study. He responded promptly. The following morning, he introduced me to the principal. After a quick test, she called the hall monitor and told him to take me to see Miss Candida, the third level teacher.

I knew the Russian alphabet that has many Latin letters. That's why I learned to read Portuguese without much effort, spelling out the names of the stores and the labels of the empty bottles I had been buying in Porto Alegre.

Miss Candida pointed to a seat, and I sat down very shyly in the midst of my new schoolmates' curiosity.

At recess, the patio filled up with a happy and boisterous rabble of students of both sexes, provoking an enormous racket around the school.

The boys ran to the end of the patio, where there were two flowering Silk Floss trees that served as natural goals for soccer, and selected players for this game. The girls, who didn't play, strolled about in groups or pairs on the walkways, conversing and laughing, their arms entwined around their waists.

I didn't know anyone except for my friend.

With the bashfulness and curiosity of a newcomer, I warily observed that childhood world from afar. And, without wanting to, I remembered that long-ago Monday morning when I was carried, sick, to the hospital on Papa's shoulders. I looked at the new world that surrounded me. That morning's dream had transformed itself into a promising reality.

No one there knew that I had loaded carcasses of meat, washed medicine bottles, sold fruit, fish, and chickens, and had pushed a handcart, buying empty bottles and cans. All that gave me a feeling of moral inferiority, had stayed behind, way behind, in the shadows of the past.

Finally, I felt equal to the others. And I watched, happily, the children that played gayly in the soft and golden morning light.

Chapter 13

The next day I woke up very early to go to school. Before I left, Mama called for me, and gave me a package.

"Take this, my son, so that you won't be hungry."

I grabbed the package without examining it. And I left, content, with my arms full of texts and notebooks.

In class, as the dictation session started, the fellow next to me, looking for a pencil under his desk, found the package that I had brought. He stealthfully opened the paper it was wrapped in and began to laugh softly, curiously staring at me like someone who was examining some weird phenomenon.

A strange feeling of unease overtook me. I realized right away that he was mocking me. I remembered the snack and Mama's words. I brought my hands under the desk and felt all over the bundle. I shuddered.

Mama had given me a whole bottle of milk and a respectable piece of bread.

With perverse pleasure, my classmate immediately transmitted this great discovery to the classmates behind us. And these, in turn, took charge of passing the news to the front. In a few minutes, the whole male section knew about the incident.

When the dictation started, I felt a slap on my shoulder. I turned around. A pimply faced boy asked me with all the seriousness in the world,

"Eh, kid, how much for a kilo of bread?"

It was as if he had stabbed me. I stared at him with an anger mixed with shame, and I returned to my previous position. I lost the train of the dictation, and I began to stir in my bench terribly ashamed, suffering a cold sweat.

Shortly, another student, remembering the bottle, asked quietly, but in a way that was heard by the classmates closest to him,

"And the milk, my friend, is it expensive?"

"If it weren't watered down," added another, "I'd take a half liter."

Muffled laughs broke out. . . .

"Silence!" the teacher exclaimed severely, ringing the bell on her desk.

Everyone bent over their notebooks, pretending to concentrate on their work.

From my desk, I sent her a look of silent and heart-felt gratitude.

I didn't know how to get out of that embarrassing situation. I counted the minutes, waiting with unnerving impatience for recess.

When the bell rang, I took a deep breath, relieved.

The students got up noisily, with an incessant dragging of feet. Pushing and shoving, they made their way outside.

I was the last to leave, carrying my snack hidden under my jacket.

I chose a quiet place on the edge of a small ravine, on an unfinished street behind the school, removed from the malicious curiosity of my classmates, and I sat down. I calmly spread a newspaper over my knees, put the piece of bread on top, unscrewed the bottle, and began to eat, thoroughly oblivious to the world. But, as I raised the bottle and bent my head a little backward to take a sip of milk, with a great and bitter surprise, my eyes fell on a group of girls laughing as they watched me from the other side of the ravine.

I lost my head. I lifted myself up and pitched the bread and the bottle into a nearby thicket of mimosa trees, gave my back to the girls, and, desolated, I tried to disappear among the other boys, swearing to myself that I would never again bring bread and milk to class.

But, a year after this shameful experience, chance made me suffer another time, the worst I can ever remember.

It was on the day of the disastrous debut of the white trousers.

I slipped them on with great delight, and happy and elegant I left for school. Almost there, I went into a grocery store to buy brown sugar candy. As there were customers in front of me and I felt a little tired from the walk, I sat down on top of a sack that was next to the counter, waiting for my turn. The purchase made, I left.

Entering the classroom, I was late. Upset with my tardiness, I sat down in my usual place and began to put my supplies in order. Just then, the teacher picked me to collect my classmates' copybooks.

The collection of copybooks was usually considered a distinction conferred on the student that stood out for his exemplary behavior or his great dedication to his studies. But receiving this honor for the first time, I attributed it, exclusively, to my new trousers.

Flattered with this honorable charge, I began to collect the books. But, as I advanced to the center of the classroom, I realized that whispers and giggles were arising and chasing me like a swarm of furious bees.

I first thought it was because of my new clothes. I noted, however, that no one in front found anything special in my clothes. It was only when they saw me from behind that the students started to laugh.

I became nervous and apprehensive. I began to worry about the cause of all this.

A classmate, taking pity on my situation, revealed to me that on the seat of my dear little pants there was an enormous black stain.

At once, I remembered the sack in the store. It was full of coal.

A wave of blood rose to my face, blurring my vision.

I tried to finish the copybook collection as quickly as possible while hiding the most vulnerable part of my body from my classmates' mocking grins.

The work finished, I sat down, shaking with impatience for recess to begin. I felt crushed by the weight of my shame.

During recess, covering the splotch on my pants with my hat, I went to the same store, bought a stick of chalk, crumbled it and covered the stain with the powder until it was invisible. Satisfied with the result, I returned to class. But, as I walked, the powder fell off, and the stain reappeared. I realized this too late, in drawing class where we were obliged to work standing up.

How much suffering that coal stain cost me!

The rest of the morning was a true hell for me. I returned home through the least traveled streets of the city.

Remembering, now, that episode of the little white trousers, I see in it a sad symbol of contemporary morals that are scandalized by a simple blot on a piece of clothing, but yet tolerate, or even raise to meritorious heights, men whose consciences are so dirty that they truly stain civilization.

Chapter 14

My friendship with a boy named Walter, who was in the final year at the same school, dates from that period in my life. For several years, his life as a poor student was intertwined with mine.

Son of a modest family of German origin who lived near us, he was a year younger than me.

We met accidentally leaving school one day. From mere classmates, our initial relationship changed rapidly into a firm friendship that has been unbreakable until today, due to an affinity of sentiments and ideas.

We were inseparable.

"You're like brothers," noted with satisfaction our mothers.

And, in fact, in spirit, we were.

With fraternal warmth, we shared our joys and sadness, our doubts and convictions. When there arose some divergence of ideas respecting certain topics that escaped our knowledge, we would discuss them as good comrades. Once the discussion was finished, we recommenced our play, without any resentment, as if nothing had passed between us.

Our favorite pastime was drawing. We also enjoyed other forms of amusement, normal to boys our age. We liked soccer and marbles, but we felt particularly attracted to drawing which gave us special satisfaction. We spent whole afternoons in the yard, lying down in the shade of the trees, copying figures and landscapes from old illustrated German magazines.

Our drawings were rated among the best in the yearly manual arts exhibit. We even nursed an inner hope to continue on to painting when we grew up. But we abandoned this dream as soon as we found out that painters usually drank, due to the fumes emanating from their paints. And that the great masters of the brush were also great drunkards.

Valuing common decency over fame won through this miserable vice, we renounced our naïve dream, placing virtue above a sullied glory.

Neither did we like brawls. Indeed, we even had an instinctive aversion to violence and brutal gestures. Whenever possible, we sought to separate friends when they got into fights, trying to persuade them that only reason had the right to settle disagreements. We avoided wild boys, troublemakers, those who started fights. We were seduced by the nobility of lofty sentiments. We were fascinated by the moral beauty of high held principles.

That's why we lived isolated, taking refuge in a world apart, dividing our time between studies and amusements, speaking of great men, expressing great admiration for the moving selflessness of those that allowed themselves to be sacrificed in defense of great humanitarian ideals.

I remember that once we carried on a heated discussion about the number of lives that would compensate for the sacrifice of ours. I thought I could give up my life to save just one hundred. My friend disagreed, alleging that was much too few and that for less than five hundred he wouldn't give up his.

Not being able to reach an agreement we finally resolved to let time clear up this transcendental dilemma.

Many years went by. My friend received his bachelor's degree, and later I did too. But until now that dilemma still is unresolved. I could only verify, with pained astonishment and abject disgust, that to maintain the luxury and leisure of useless individuals, thousands and thousands of precious lives have been sacrificed.

My friend played the violin. His only sister, the piano.

Many times, in summer, when the excessive heat forced us to stay inside, they would play together an excerpt of classical music or a sentimental Viennese waltz.

Their mother would stop her domestic chores within another part of the house, wipe her hands on her apron, and come silently to sit in the living room next to her children to listen to them. She sat contemplating them with the satisfaction and pride of someone who admires the beauty of a grand arduously realized dream and feels fully compensated for the hardships endured.

With thongs on his feet, black knickers above his knees, a white wide collared shirt open to his chest, his chin firmly resting on the violin, his head slightly inclined towards the left, with one hand securing the violin, the other the bow and his gaze fixed on the sheet of music, my friend played, marking the rhythm with his foot. His fingers either skipped over the cords with agility or honored them with a slow quivering pace as the bow rose and fell, at times rapidly, at times leisurely.

By his side, her chest a little bent over the piano, her long thick blonde braids falling down her back, his sister ran her fingers over the piano keys, accompanying him. Near them, motionless, abstracted, lost in deep meditation, was their mother, enraptured with the music. But when they played a languid and sentimental waltz, she began to accompany them, quietly singing in German. Her soft voice, infused with great gentleness and intense emotion, seemed to lull us into deep nostalgia.

Moved by the beauty of that family scene, that the music made almost sublime, I couldn't help but contrast the charm of that simple life with our life of melancholy.

I never heard my mother sing. She was always sad, depressed, pining away, and complaining of her fate.

However, even in poverty, there could be rejoicing.

I remembered a used violin that I had seen abandoned in our store. And I was filled with an immense desire to learn to play that instrument.

One day, playing marbles with Walter, in the courtyard of his house, I shared with him this wish, asking him if he would teach me the violin. He agreed most willingly and began to teach me the art that, later, for some months, would earn me my daily bread.

Chapter 15

Upon finishing my studies at *Colégio Elementar*, I enrolled immediately in a night school commercial course founded and directed by the teacher I studied with during the last year of primary school.

It is with consummate reverence that I here recall the beloved figure of my former teacher, the first friend that encouraged me to take the entrance exams for an institution of higher learning.

Of medium height, slender, bald, with a wide forehead, lively black eyes, a tan and shaven face, an ancient Roman profile, an elegant almost military gait, he shaped the fine characters of several generations during the long years that he served as an educator.

Friend to his students, he always showed a truly paternal concern for their futures.

One night, I arrived early to class. The other students hadn't come yet. My teacher shook his legs nervously, waiting for them.

I sat down, opened a book, and started to read.

"Paulo," he asked me all of a sudden, "are you planning to follow a commercial trade?"

"I don't know yet."

"You should study engineering. You like mathematics. And you have a certain facility with numbers."

I thanked him for his complimentary words. But with the arrival of my classmates, we interrupted our conversation.

Leaving the classroom, the memory of my teacher's words came back to me.

I had just a year left before I would finish the bookkeeping course. What would I do afterward? What opportunities would the knowledge of commercial accounting open up for me? An obscure job in some commercial establishment and a mediocre future. I would spend my days, months, and years, perhaps all my life, closed up in dreary offices, writing entries and balances in a rounded and careful hand. I felt desolated by the sheer idea of wasting my life filling blank books with the comings and goings of merchandise. And dressing up beef jerky, black beans, lard, and onions with a pretty and elegant script.

Despite my Semitic blood, I didn't have any ambition for wealth. The prestige of money did not seduce me. A finer one, the prestige of learning, fascinated me. I mainly studied to acquire knowledge, and better comprehend life, to have a clear notion of things, to understand the formation and workings of the world with the detailed assurance of a technician who intimately understands the mechanisms and operation of the most complicated machine.

That's why, when later on I received my bookkeeping diploma, I accepted my instructor's suggestion and, without taking into account the fragility of the economic ground I was treading, I worked on mathematics with him and went to Porto Alegre to take the exam on this subject.

Seeing Porto Alegre again, a raft of stray memories came to my mind.

I remembered the night we arrived from the farming settlement and remained in the deserted station not knowing which way to go. I remembered the winter mornings when I delivered meat with Daniel, the time when Papa sold fish, Solon sweets, and Luiz ice cream. I felt a certain type of pride that now I had come with the hope of one day entering an Academy.

I lodged in the room of a friend from Santa Maria, today a medical doctor with a brilliant future and, back then, a senior bookkeeper with the State railway company.

I arrived a month before the exams to have enough time to review the material. And I threw myself enthusiastically into my studies.

Weeks before the exam, at a charity event, I met a girl named Sonia, who made a profound impression on me. When our looks crossed for the first time, I gazed at her shyly, without any hope of return. So it caused me incredible surprise to realize that every once in a while she was sending me meaningful smiles.

Enlivened with an unusual boldness, I took advantage of the "secret message" service that was part of the party's entertainment, and I sent her a card with the following phrases if my memory doesn't fail me: "Will it be a crime to love? But to love as one loves the sun, only for the warmth it gives. Without the insane hope of touching it one day."

She read it and turned around to smile at me, without thinking of how a simple sympathetic smile could affect a boy in my circumstances.

I never had a sister, a natural outlet for my emotions. I exited childhood, never coddled, my soul saturated with suffering and grief, distilled by poverty, alcohol, and humiliation. I felt a dire need for affection. For kind words. For a little bit of happiness, having yet not known any.

That's why her smile quickly overpowered me. And all my repressed feelings and desires burst out with extraordinary force, casting me into the whirlpool of a grand romantic passion.

I spent that night and the subsequent days constantly thinking of Sonia. I couldn't forget her, not even for a moment.

Rejoicing with happiness, I took the exam at the Julio de Castilhos High School, and I passed. I had decided to study engineering.

I wasn't attracted to medicine. Nor was I attracted to Law because I considered it a low-level career. I believed that, as a rule, lying and chicanery were fundamental to its success. So, I was left with my teacher's advice. I decided to follow it based on a naïve conviction that we all have free will. However, I was convinced of the contrary later on when I was obliged, for financial reasons and at a great personal loss, to abandon the career I preferred, in exchange for Law. Begrudgingly, I went on to receive a Bachelor of Law degree.

Chapter 16

I returned to Santa Maria, deeply in love.

I couldn't forget Sonia, who came to dominate my whole being with the strength of a genuine obsession.

Her image never left me, not even for a second. I saw her in everything and everywhere. She was on the page of the book that I opened. On the blank sheets of paper that I touched. In the paleness of the moon and in the radiance of the stars. I sensed her soul in the perfume of the flowers. And I felt her hands in the caress of the breeze.

She encompassed, in my enamored eyes, all that was most beautiful in the world. And, in this world, for me, only she existed. I couldn't bear life without the enchantment of her presence. And I felt capable of committing the greatest follies in response to the slightest wave of her hand.

I pronounced her name with a trembling heart. With true veneration, I evoked her image, which never abandoned me. And, overwhelmed with love and longing, I studied enthusiastically, awaiting with anxious impatience the next exam period that would allow me to see her again.

Already elated, anticipating the pleasure of being with her, the year-end's arrival brought me one of the purest and loftiest joys of my life.

When, once back in Porto Alegre, I turned the corner onto the street where she lived, I almost fainted from excitement, realizing that in a few minutes I would be by her side.

Her welcoming embrace enveloped me in an intense wave of emotion, filling my heart with the invisible lava of a volcanic passion.

From then on, I spent my days in cock-eyed bliss, as if I were the happiest of mortals. I lived in a world apart, constantly dazed.

I visited her every night and then would return, happy, to my room, with my heart overflowing with love. That's why, as soon as I entered my lodgings, an unshakable yearning, an enormous urge to see her again overtook me. I couldn't study anymore. A tremendous conflict arose, a fierce internal fight, between duty and desire. The former ordered me to stay home and study. The latter, which sought its beloved, pushed me toward the street. And I ended up going out the door.

Meanwhile, the exam dates were growing closer. Only some weeks more and they would be here. And I hadn't yet begun my review. The dark cloud of a failing grade terrified me. Futilely, I tried to react, to reconcile the demands of duty with my capricious emotions. However, my heart that had taken complete hold of me was always the victor in this conflict.

Many times, after getting ready to go out, my conscience protested, reproaching me. Then, repentant, I went back on my decision, undressed, put on my pajamas, sat down at the table, and opened a book with the firm intention not to leave it until I mastered everything that would be on the exam.

But, while my eyes passed over the pages, my thoughts were flying back to Sonia's house, and there they remained, conversing with her at the little iron gate. Then I saw her seated with me in the parlor, next to a table covered with a red velvet cloth. From the vase that rested on the table, fresh daisies tumbled out, smiling.

When I got to the end of the page, I no longer remembered what I had read at the beginning. Sonia absorbed me completely. I tried to forget her, to put her away from my thoughts and to concentrate all my attention on the book. But all my efforts were pointless, all my attempts useless.

I closed the book, desperate. And I started to walk nervously around the room searching for a solution to this situation that now was seriously worrying me.

After many false starts, I landed on an effective remedy.

In the morning I entered the barbershop and ordered my hair cut with the electric razor, as close as possible. The barber, with a skeptical smile, thinking that it was a joke, picked up the scissors and the comb to cut my hair as usual.

Right away I protested, reiterating my order in all seriousness. The barber no longer had doubts. He substituted the razor for the scissors, shaving my entire head, leaving my whole skull on view.

The way I looked, I no longer had any desire to go and see Sonia. When I looked at myself in the mirror, my passionate ardor withered completely. And I felt in my heart what Samson of the biblical legend felt in his muscles after Delilah's betrayal. . . .

Only like this did I manage to stay home and study with my spirits at ease. And this confinement that I had imposed on myself served its purpose.

I passed my exams. But, I confess, they were the most expensive exams of my life. Besides the inscription fees, they also cost me a head of hair. . . .

Chapter 17

At home, business began to unravel.

The sales and our purchases were declining. And as merchandise sold, there appeared large empty spaces on the once well-stocked shelves.

Papa went about worried, with a furrowed brow, as he leaned over the counter to examine invoices, making calculations on sheets of brown wrapping paper and noting the due dates for debts. Then, he would go to the door to look out at similar establishments, the stores of his rivals.

When by chance he saw customers entering or leaving his competitors' shops, carrying purchases in their arms, he felt somewhat injured. And he started to walk around the store, pensive. Other times he would pass his eyes over the shelves, forming a mental inventory of the stock.

To stabilize the situation, he started a grocery section. His excessive goodness, however, wouldn't let him refuse to sell on credit, which caused him serious harm.

His financial situation, already precarious, then became even more delicate due to the arrival of an unforeseen circumstance.

One morning fire broke out in our neighbor's general store. The light of the flames and the ringing of the fire bells brought to the scene of the disaster an enormous crowd of the curious.

The blazing flames spread with horrifying speed, threatening to lick the roof of our establishment.

"Throw out the goods," shouted some in the crowd.

Unnerved and out of his mind from this imminent danger, Papa agreed to let his merchandise be thrown out all jumbled up into the middle of the street, where it suffered serious damage.

The fire didn't spread. But our losses were considerable. And, from that morning on, Papa began to drink again.

I, however, unaware of our true financial state, headed to Porto Alegre at the end of the year to take the exams that would be held in February.

Shortly before then, my friend Walter, who had completed his studies in Santa Maria, had also gone to Porto Alegre to prepare for the Law School entrance exam and he installed himself in the room that I had occupied.

As there wasn't room for both of us and to avoid being separated, as well as to save our landlord the loss of a boarder, I suggested that a room be built for us in the back yard, as both Walter and I were planning to remain in Porto Alegre to continue our studies. The landlord agreed to the proposal and had the room built. It was soon ready.

It was a wooden shed, covered with tiles, with a door and two glassless windows, exposed walls, and no interior divisions. But it had room to spare for two people.

We moved in just as thrilled as if we were about to inhabit a sumptuous palace. In that shed, there was space for all our dreams.

Then we eagerly threw ourselves into our studies.

I continued visiting Sonia every night, and my life went along happily between my studies and my love.

But it happened that Sonia had a sister, younger than her, named Ilsa. I had seen her for the first time on a tram, without knowing who she was. And the cute little figure she cut caught my attention. Especially, her blonde hair.

Quite a few times she remained in the small nut-colored pine sitting room where we conversed, taking part in our long idyllic evenings. With time, I became captivated by the gold of her lovely hair and the grace she radiated. And I ended up falling in love with her too, so I now loved both sisters. I couldn't think of one without at the same time remembering the other. In my dreams they complemented one another, forming a single ideal image. With equal passion, my heart fluttered in concert, for both. And, in this sweet state of good fortune, I lived for several years, receiving as a divine gift the favor of their affection.

Without money and, sometimes, without bread, fighting constantly with adversity, I found in the tenderness of those two good creatures the breaths of strength that kept me from giving in to the despair that frequently overtook me. I knew, I even had total certainty, that later on, we would take different paths in life. At no moment did I even cherish the least illusion in this respect. Nevertheless, I loved them fervently.

But I never let fall from my lips a word of love or an indirect confession of my passion. We spoke of everything except me. And perhaps without their knowing, I remained, in large part, in their debt, for the energy I gleaned to maintain the fight and for the happy hours of spiritual kinship that I stored for eternity in the bottom of my poor and grateful heart.

Chapter 18

One afternoon, coming back from my classes, right on the street, an acquaintance of ours who had arrived the night before from Santa Maria gave me a letter from my father, confessing our family's financial ruin and the consequent impossibility of forwarding me the monthly allowance for my studies.

Reading the letter filled me with great sadness and left me entirely disoriented. For the first time in my life, I was alone in a big city, without any resources and without knowing what to do.

I was seized with an immense feeling of dejection. I started to walk aimlessly, thinking of my situation and my family's. And, drifting along, without any specific route, I arrived at praça da Matriz. I sat down on a bench, trying to find in the silent loneliness of that quiet corner of the city, some way to climb out of the state of complete helplessness to which I had been abruptly reduced.

My first impulse was to return to Santa Maria, find employment in a commercial establishment, and be by my family's side.

I had, however, a real passion for my studies and I couldn't accept the thought of abandoning them, a thought that threw me into despair. That's why I thought the best choice would be to stay and find work in Porto Alegre. But, on the other hand, I didn't really want to trade my time for a miserable wage. Just thinking of this made me suffer terribly. I struggled to find a formula capable of reconciling work and study. I would rather undergo the greatest hardships than part with my books. But, as much as I tried to find it, I couldn't discover a way to earn a living without affecting my studies. The sight of a priest who was leisurely making his way up the hill on rua General Camara gave me an idea for solving my anguished situation: enter a seminary.

Without material worries, I could study at will. I would have peace. A good bed. A full table. Good wine. Spiritual tranquility. And a silence permeated with unperturbed religiosity inviting long and fruitful meditations. Before taking the habit, I would loyally confess my lack of vocation for the ecclesiastical life, and so recuperate my freedom, carrying with me, in exchange for years of voluntary seclusion, a considerable store of knowledge that would enable me to triumph in life with greater ease.

Excited by this idea, I rose from the bench, having decided to carry out my plan. With firm resolution, I directed my steps towards the rua Espirito Santo, where I supposed the seminary was located.

Arriving at the wide and heavy iron gate that isolated it from the world, I stopped undecided.

The sight of the high, thick, and solid walls that surrounded the building, which I mistakenly thought was the seminary, and the austere and tombstone silence that reigned within, cooled my enthusiasm and made me reflect at length on the consequences of the decision I had taken.

Nightfall was approaching. And the sun was a song of light on the concave blue of the sky. A great and soft serenity hovered in this bluish transparency of the air, gently wrapping the earth in a wide and loving embrace. Immersed in their perpetual immobility as they reflected the daylight, the mountains were trimmed with a luminous halo of pale gold. Over the still and shimmering waters of the Guaíba River, the sun's rays dissolved into thousands of golden sparkles. Everywhere there was a wonderful combination of gold and blue, of light and shadow, offering marvelous panels that were constantly changing under the divine spell of the setting sun.

Through the air, languished a voluptuous numbing warmth while the distant bustle of the city calmly waned. And the infinite and beneficent peace that descended gently from the sky was mystically married with the sublime sweetness that placidly rose from the ground.

The life that embraced me, throbbing with dreams and beauty, was too lovely to be buried in the cold sterility of a monastery. I asked myself if it were worth the sacrifice of the best years of my youth to acquire a fistful of knowledge, whose value I was totally unsure of.

I didn't lack the courage to renounce the world. But I had great doubts about the advantage of trading my freedom for a prison, even a temporary one.

This and other considerations made me desist from my plan. And I went back along the same road, with the firm intention not to leave Porto Alegre, ready to fight adversity face to face.

By the time I arrived home, night had fully descended.

Noting my dismay, my friend Walter tried to find out why I was upset. I told him what was bothering me.

He wrinkled his forehead and remained pensive for a few moments. Then he asked:

"Have you taken a decision?"

"I have," I responded dryly as if it were painful for me to speak.

"What do you plan to do?" he insisted, with concern.

"Work during the day and study at night."

He scratched his head.

"I think that will be difficult . . . almost unworkable."

"Why?"

"In engineering, as you know, class attendance is mandatory. And I don't see how you can satisfy this requirement if you are working."

"But until then," I objected, "I still have plenty of time ahead."

"No, my friend. You need to anticipate everything, starting now. It might be that later your situation could grow much worse. We should face things without being overly optimistic."

A grave and heavy silence enveloped us.

"I can't find another solution to my problem," I argued, to justify my decision.

"Why don't you change careers?" he suggested.

"Change careers?" I repeated puzzled, surprised at his suggestion.

"Yes, choose another one," clarified my friend. "Unfortunately, you didn't want to listen to me when I advised you a while ago to follow the profession that I chose, trying to convince me that Law rested on arbitrary concepts. And that only engineering, and medicine, and the areas related to them were based on scientific principles. Let's not discuss now, whether or not the Law is a science, or try to establish a hierarchical scale for the liberal professions measuring their greater or lesser value as a social good. Since you can't follow your true vocation, your only course is to leave aside your preferences and opt for a career that can assure you a more or less secure future. Now, becoming a lawyer seems the best route. Attendance at Law School is optional. You can attend classes when you please and only have to miss work each year on the final exam days."

"Yes, but the exams I have been preparing to take at Julio de Castilhos, as you know, aren't valid for Law School."

"It doesn't matter. Drop them and start everything over again. In three or four years, maximum, you can finish the humanities course, and you can enter Law School, while, if you insist in studying engineering, you could perhaps repent too late. Right now, you're still in time."

My friend's advice encouraged me. His considerations were sensible. I took the time to measure and weigh them carefully, reaching the sad conclusion that, contrary to what we think, our will is no more than a simple plaything in the capricious and inexorable hands of fate.

My friend awaited my decision, observing the effect his words had on me.

I was undecided, pulled by opposing feelings and desires.

I paced around the room and stopped in front of the window.

Outside, there was an endless calm wrapped in the night's silence. Yet, how much anguish, how much suffering, and how many voiceless desires did that apparent tranquility encircle?

Finally, after much reflection, I turned towards my friend who continued to watch me while seated at the table, drumming a pencil on an open notebook. I went up to him with serene resolve, and I said, holding out my hand:

"Let's shake. And from today on, consider me your future colleague," I added, smiling.

"May you be happy!" he responded, giving me a strong hand shake full of the warmth of an old friendship.

Some eight years later, more or less, on a cold July night, I solemnly received from the Free Law School of Porto Alegre, with other classmates of my year, the bachelor's degree in judicial and social sciences, repeating, in Latin, the hallowed words of the official oath.

I had fulfilled, religiously, the promise made to my friend, without, though, having managed to modify my previous opinion of the career I was obliged to follow. . . .

Chapter 19

For two long weeks, that seemed two centuries, I looked for work.

In our mind's clock, the hands of suffering and the hands of pleasure do not move at the same rate. While the latter turn with the dizzy speed of bliss, the others move with the tyrannical slowness of torture. But for those looking for work, time seems to stand still in the sensuous sadism of a morbid pleasure.

Goaded by need, and pushed by the desire to partake in the communion of human dignity that work would allow, I lived in silent desperation under the crushing pressure of an enormous feeling of inferiority.

Above all, the unemployed are great sufferers.

For the righteous crime of being honest and healthy, they are condemned to the humiliating sentence of begging for employment. Of going hungry among abundance. Of going forth ragged amidst luxury. Of enduring, in essence, every hardship, within the boundless prison of their own freedom.

I went out every morning. I would go to the center of the city. I would buy a newspaper. I would take refuge in a deserted corner of the praça da Alfandega, or in an unobtrusive nook in some café, looking for any employment as I avidly read from top to bottom, from the first to the last line, the classified ad pages, which magically created great, if ephemeral, hopes that were born in full bloom each morning, wilted during the day, and always died with the coming of night.

Tired of searching, not hopeful of finding anything, I was taking my dejection to the cafes, to drown it in the tumultuous waves of life that constantly entered and left by the wide-open doors. And putting on a carefree air, so as not to show to the indifferent eyes of the world the silent despair that gnawed at my heart, I spent hours and hours in front of a small cup of coffee viewing, without seeing, the life that was steaming around me, because my eyes were turned towards the depths of my own suffering.

In the deepest layers of the human soul exist unconscious remnants of an ancestral fatalism, which, in the unemployed, take on special proportions and significance. That's why, when they see their last chances to find work fail and realize that changes to their miserable situations are out of their control, they give up their destinies to the whimsical play of circumstances. To the blind chain of events. To the variable sequence of days. And they await, with impatient anguish, the slow roll out of developments, in the hope of finding their salvation in merely accidental surprises.

It was waiting like this, at a secluded table in a café that a friend came to tell me of an opening in the offices of the Railroad Cooperative.

With generous concern, he took me there immediately, and I received an appointment as a clerk in the accounting department.

I worked with another clerk who exhibited, in his servile attitude, his timid gestures, his resigned voice, his sad features, his kind expression, and his body bent from more than fifteen years of a sedentary and monotonous life, the defeated air of a poor and humble public servant.

My task consisted of spending my days in the sad silence of a stark room summing up long and massive columns of numbers.

I threw myself into the work with enormous enthusiasm. But, little by little, the enthusiasm gave way to despondency.

The enervating monotony of the interminable repetition of this mediocre task deflated my spirit to a state of complete ennui. The obligatory immobility unnerved me. The tiny digits produced the burning sensation of biting ants. I carried out my calculations with annoyance, mechanically. I felt a lack of air. Of light. Of life. I was exasperated.

Like a convict, I looked at the world that pulsated on the luminous rectangle of the window. At the free flight of the birds, drawing peaceful curves in the vast blue of the sky. At the white expanse of the sails that the wind softly propelled across the resplendent surface of the Guaíba waters. At the puffing trains that arrived and departed filling the streets and crackling the air with the bronzed resonance of the measured ring of their bells.

Life outside glowed in the triumphal beauty of clear sky days. And there I was, inside, in this bureaucratic tomb, leaning over a table full of invoices, adding up the portions of each bill from morning to night.

The slow dry tick-tock of the wall clock marking, within the austere atmosphere that surrounded me, the somber flow towards the vacuum of eternity, of the seconds of every minute, the minutes of every hour, the hours of every day, almost drove me crazy. I anguished over the precious time that the insatiable numbers devoured. Every sum took away a portion of my own existence. When I thought of this, I felt a repressed protest from my imprisoned freedom, a wave of internal revolt, rise from the depths of my being to die, strangled, in the silent impotence of clinched fingers.

Each morning I ripped off the department's daily work schedule with a mangled soul as if I were ripping off, bleeding, a piece of my own life.

I lived anxious, distressed, thinking of a way to liberate myself from that terrible situation.

The sudden death of the wife of the owner of our shed ignited in me a real feeling for the brevity of life, which heightened, even more, my despair.

A few days after this death, my friend Walter moved to another boarding house. I remained behind.

Since I felt sorry to wake the eldest orphan to make a fire, I went out some mornings without breakfast. I bought crackers on my way to work, and I ate them furtively in the office.

"Don't let the boss surprise you chewing here," my colleague warned me one day.

"But I can't work if I fast."

"You haven't had breakfast yet?"

"No, I didn't. I live far away. So as not to miss the bus, I sometimes come without breakfast."

"That's not good for you."

"What can I do?"

He kept quiet. Then, somewhat constrained, he made a suggestion,

"At home, I have an empty room. It is very close to here, at praça Florida. If you like it, I can let you have it."

After work, I went with him to see the accommodation that was close to the Cooperative. When we arrived at his house, from the sidewalk, he pointed out a shed in the back of the yard, explaining that it was the room he had mentioned, which used to be his son's before he left for Rio.

Noticing my surprise, he added:

"It's not very comfortable. But, in return, you will have more than enough time for breakfast. From here to work is a short jump."

I didn't care about comfort. I thought of the periodic fasts imposed by distance. Of the slope on rua Ramiro Barcellos that I had to mount two times a day. That's why, without looking inside, I decided to rent the room. And, that very same night, I put my ramshackle belongings in a wagon—a fold up cot, a table, a chair and some books and I climbed up. I arranged a place for myself, and I sat down being very careful to secure the kerosene lamp so the tube wouldn't break.

The wagon driver lit the candle in the lantern that hung from the front of the vehicle, and a small pale and flickering light twinkled in the darkness of rua Francisco Ferrer, at that time, perhaps the narrowest and most pothole ridden street in Porto Alegre. Then he tapped the horse with the whip, and the wagon started off.

I was immensely sorry to leave that poor and peaceful little street where the most precious dreams of my youth had blossomed and to where, later on, I would return to live.

There are certain streets that are inseparably tied to our destinies. You can say that they become an integral part of our lives because on these streets occur, almost always, the most important events of our existence.

For me, Francisco Ferrer was one of those streets.

I could never forget it, and I always recall it with longing, despite the bitter times I later went through there.

When the wagon pulled up at the sidewalk curb in front of my colleague's house, he came out and helped me unload my things and put them in the shed that he had kindly offered me.

Once I was alone, I lit the lamp and passed my eyes around the room.

It was an abandoned shed. The wooden walls were almost totally covered with old newspapers, completely yellowed by time. Some, just barely attached at only one spot, swayed at the least puff of air, like enormous, foreboding wings. Others, having fallen from the walls, were spread out on the floor. The flooring didn't even have two flush boards, and it creaked under my steps. And everywhere, there were great big spider webs covered with dust.

I stood still, desolated, looking at the wretchedness that surrounded me. And I felt in my soul a cold shadow of abandonment and loneliness.

I set up the cot and arranged my things the best I could. Then not being able to put up any longer with the immense sadness that invaded me, I went out, to the house of the two sisters, to forget the painful impact of the room in the sweet shelter of their friendship. And I only returned after midnight.

The next day, I had breakfast in a restaurant on rua Cristovão Colombo where I had started to have my meals, paying for them daily, after dinner. But, soon afterward, my calculations showed me that the money I had wouldn't last until I received my first paycheck.

To balance my precarious financial situation, I resolved to restrict my spending, sustaining myself until the end of the month just on coffee with lots of milk, at two cafes that are next to each other in front of the railroad station, Independencia and Nacional.

In order not to expose my destitute state to the waiters, I had coffee one day at the Independencia and the next day at the Nacional. And so on, alternating.

"Breakfast, at this hour?" exclaimed, with astonishment, a friend who caught me once, as I was having coffee with bread and butter at midday.

"Doctor's orders," I responded somewhat embarrassed. But, once I recovered myself, I added in a loud voice so that the waiter that was looking at me could hear:

"I am suffering from stomach problems. And the doctor recommended a strict diet."

It seems that both believed in my illness.

Slowly, I adapted to this new system of nourishment and my uncomfortable room.

I didn't receive any visits from friends because I didn't give them my address. I was ashamed to show them where I lived.

And I continued on like this, motivated by a strong premonition that all that would pass and that better days were to come.

One night, when the weather seemed to be bringing rain, I decided to stay in the room, and I started to read.

All of a sudden, a violent storm fell over the city.

A gust of wind ripped off the newspapers, whistling eerily through the wide gaps in the walls. Great drops of water began to strike the table. A crisp pop, from breaking glass, toppled half of the lantern's tube onto the book that I was reading. The other half remained in the lantern that started to smolder, giving everything a mournful tinge.

I moved the table to a better place. But the leaks multiplied, rapidly. Water ran down the walls, under the door, just everywhere.

I arranged a more or less dry space for the bed and, beaten by weariness and dejection, I lay down and slept.

The next day I woke up very cold. Part of the pillow and the blanket were wet. The books, spread out on the floor and table, were soaked through and through. The wood flooring was swamped. And the room had the desolate look of a real flood.

Distressed and sad, I got up. I put on the wet shoes, opened the window and looked out.

Next to my miserable shed stood a pretty and elegant bungalow that was occupied by only one person, the expensive mistress of a high-level official of the Railroad Company.

The day was ugly, and the sky was full of clouds so low that they seemed to obliterate everything.

I was shivering and felt unwell. I was feverish with a heavy head and burning eyes.

I decided not to go to the office and went back to bed.

It began to rain again. And the wind began to blow. There was more wind than rain. Grim hissing sounds entered through the cracks in the walls.

The fever rose continually. Then came a cough.

I felt alone and abandoned.

Not even a little patch of blue in the sky to gladden my febrile eyes.

In the room, everything gave off a sense of dreariness. My most familiar things withdrew, stood apart, and moved away, becoming distinct entities. Each one gave the vivid impression of autonomy, of having its own life, determined, selfish. And this impression augmented my feeling of loneliness even more. The loneliness of both body and soul.

The cough, harsh and raucous, wasn't leaving me. My throat felt on fire. My hands grew warmer and warmer. And my pulse beat violently.

A bunch of memories came to me, as my thoughts swiftly crossed over one another, shuffling themselves into a strange disarray.

Drops of water began to beat to the rhythm of the rain that stopped and then went on.

Little droplet, little droplet, I murmured, how sad is your muffled tempo. Every drop is a blow to my heart.

You came, little droplet, with your sad throbbing to humbly set to music the dreariness of my poor room.

And in my head, I was reciting,

Little droplet, melancholy,
Life was always so.
Grave rhythm, monotony,
All in life reach their close.

Little droplet, why do you sob?
As I did, hide your tears
And go on singing, little one,
So they'll think you full of cheer.

Little droplet, melancholy,
Life was so always,
For just at the start of this world
Abel by Cain was slain.

And the wind lashed the rain. And the tired rain began to fall again, accelerating the rhythm of its drops while I implored,

Little droplet, why do you sob
And not let me peacefully lie?
Have pity, dry up your tears,
Or you will my sorrows revive

It was the rising fever. . . .

Chapter 20

One of the things that worried me very much at that time, and indeed had been seriously worrying me since the moment I physiologically became a man, was the whole question of sexuality.

When I began to be tortured by this innate instinct, my ignorance in respect to this delicate and complex issue was, unfortunately, complete, which led me to resolve it through the harmful practice that inevitably lays hold, but with rare exceptions, on all boys who cross the stunning and dangerous threshold of puberty.

Intuitively, I felt that I was doing wrong. And I tried to fight back, with all my strength. But neither my religious training nor my moral education managed to silence the sexual roar that grew stronger and stronger.

Educated in the old principles of the Jewish religion, I scrupulously observed its sacred commandments. I was a pure young man, both in body and mind, full of elevated feelings and ideas. That's why I felt true repugnance for my own being every time I gave in to the temptations of sin, after a useless battle, after futile resistance.

What arrested my steps on this dangerous road that I was following was a book on sexuality by a Jewish writer that was recommended to me by a friend.

Reading this work struck me to my core and was of great help in saving me from the abyss which ignorance, false modesty, and adolescent passion were irresistibly dragging me towards.

The revelation of the woes, of the grave consequences of the unnatural satisfaction of sexual desire, truly horrified me. A tremendous conflict waged inside me, a fierce fight between the uncontrollable impulses of my instincts and the powerless protests of my conscience, causing me to suffer the same anguish and moral distress that is generally experienced by all those who don't receive any sexual education.

I hold, as a truth incapable of being honestly contested, that the brakes of morality and religion are unable to clamp down on sex. For this reason, and for the dreadful and, sometimes, irreparable consequences that result from keeping adolescents sexually ignorant, I consider truly criminal the conduct of parents that follow this course, consciously, forsaking their children in the most delicate and important phase of their existence.

Influenced by a defective education, constrained by a false shame, manifestly incompatible with contemporary life, they leave their children to their own fate and lack the courage to point out the true road to follow. They forget that, beginning with its first manifestations, sexuality plays a vitally important role in an individual's subsequent normal development! Instead, these parents leave their children exposed to the chance hazards of simple circumstances.

They don't try to enter the intimate life of their children to listen to their hearts, their secret wishes, their unvoiced desires, abandoning them precisely when they most need their parents' teachings, advice, experience, and assistance.

The same thing, unfortunately, can be observed in schools, where nothing is taught on this subject. Meanwhile, a solution to the question of sexuality is needed with pressing urgency given the incalculable number of victims this ignorance has caused.

In spite of sexuality being of vital importance for the individual and, consequently, for the species itself, those responsible for the destinies of our generation, and of those that will follow, still don't dare to look it straight in the face and proclaim publicly the immediate need to find a solution. Their reticence is especially troublesome now that science has uncovered a large part of the mystery that surrounded sexuality, finding the origin of many conjugal tragedies, of many mental illnesses, and of certain crimes, which could have been prevented through rational sexual education based on scientific findings.

If we were to examine, in light of statistical data, the number of victims that the anachronism of the prevailing morality has dragged into insanity and crime and the number of lives wasted by false preconceptions, we would be truly astonished.

Animal life appeared on the face of the earth many centuries before the different ethical systems created by man and obeys, in its evolutionary march, survival and reproductive instincts. Thus, it is human society's duty, for its own sake, to continuously align moral norms with the uncontrollable demands of these instincts.

But, since, indisputably, as a rule, except for some isolated voices, sexuality has not merited the attention that it demands, it has now become urgent to scientifically realign the fundamental laws of human nature with those of social morality in order to harmonize them with the lofty and sacred interests of society and, consequently, with the interests of the species itself.

It was a lady of the night that ripped off, with French aloofness, the veil of the sexual mystery that covered my eyes.

One evening when I was returning from the public library, a woman invitingly called out to me,

"Enter, my dear."

Unsettled, I slowed my steps, gazing at her.

Leaning over the windowsill, with her breasts almost uncovered, and her eyes brightly shining, she smiled. Noting my hesitation, she repeated the invitation,

"Enter, my dear."

The vision of the white flesh of her breasts made my blood race to my head. My heart began to beat violently, but I didn't manage to conquer my timidity, and I continued walking, slowly, once again governed by opposing feelings fighting desperately inside me. Finally, when I found myself near the first corner, I decided to return, and in fact, I did go back, affecting an air of calmness and looking very carefully on all sides to make sure that no one I knew was nearby and that no one was observing me.

The woman was still in the window. I pushed the door and went in with the same sensation as someone who is throwing himself into an abyss.

I was burning up. A sudden rush of fear shook my whole body. My temples pounded with incredible force. I felt the vibrations of a strange world deep inside me. I hungered to clasp in my arms a naked woman's body. And my imagination charged my senses, heightening the pleasure of this revelation. I trembled, extremely excited and impatient. My senses were ablaze, turning me into a live flame.

....
....
....
....
....

I left disappointed. I couldn't understand why such a banal act was wrapped up in so much mystery . . . .

It was one more disillusion that I reaped from life, and I had the impression that others were still reserved for me.

Later on, through analysis based on the personal experience I was acquiring from the world of men, I reached the pessimistic conclusion that, logically, we cannot justify the sacrifices existence demands. And that the animal will to live rested on premises that still escaped my knowledge.

Why do we live and for what?

I looked for the answer in books and I threw myself with real voracity into my reading in the hope of increasing my knowledge little by little and one day seeing clearly the startling complexity of the world that surrounded me, that I was ardently attempting to comprehend, with the same clarity that I assumed the men leading the world across the centuries had viewed it.

But only much later did I recognize how much naïveté there had been in my assumption. . . .

It was from that moment on that I began to feel the tragedy of existence being born in my soul.

Chapter 21

One day, the news began to circulate that our department would be transferred to the city of Santa Maria. I was very happy about the move, which shortly took place.

In Santa Maria, I went to live with my family that had moved to a less expensive house, on the same street, where my father continued running a small store.

Business went from bad to worse. And our future held out bleak prospects which filled us all with apprehension as, resignedly, we sadly awaited the unrolling of events.

My passion for learning didn't cool off. Much to the contrary, it became even more ardent. The more that my work in the railroad cooperative took me from my books, the more forcefully I tried to hold onto them, my only lifeline.

I accepted less and less my situation. I had to spend the whole day in the office, stupidly wasting my life in the monotonous and tiresome repetition of the same transactions, which I now just performed automatically, almost mechanically.

And I didn't have enough time left to take full advantage of my studies, which upset me tremendously.

I thought about a way to harmonize my studies with my work. The only solution I found was to go to bed right after dinner, sleep for a few hours, and pass the rest of the night in camaraderie with my books.

And that's what I did.

Right after returning from work, I had dinner and went to bed. I got up more or less at midnight. The internal partitions of our house went only halfway up the wooden walls and my brothers and I all slept in the same room that the electric lamp in the sitting room illuminated. So in order not to wake them I lit a candle and went to study quietly behind a wardrobe where I had placed a chair and a small table. And I remained there, half asleep, in the great silence of the night, devouring pages under the flickering light of the flame.

Not always, however, did I manage to wake up at the desired hour. Many times, I came home tired and soon plunged into such a deep sleep that I only woke up the next day. Other times sleep abandoned me. Then,

I would make desperate attempts to capture it. I would pin my eyes on a fixed point. I would mentally add up incredible sums, counting until I was exhausted. But to no effect. Sleep only arrived a little before the hour set for my vigil and I only just woke up in time to go to work.

I appealed to Mother, asking her to wake me just after midnight, in case I was still sleeping. She promised she would. But when the time arrived to fulfill the promise it pained her to rouse me, and she let me sleep, which distressed me immensely.

To remedy the situation, I turned to drink.

Before lying down, I would ingest a large dose of alcohol, trying to become quite woozy so I could fall asleep. But I would wake up sick with violent headaches. After various attempts, I realized that this method wouldn't produce the desired effect.

Thus, the unsatisfactory result of drinking and the fear of the consequences of the immoderate use of alcohol led me to abandon this dangerous remedy that I was using to get out of a desperate situation. Since my health had begun to resent the wakeful nights, the days of exhausting work and the excesses of alcohol, I was forced to finally take an extreme measure, leave my job.

Liberating myself became my greatest concern, acquiring the proportions and the commanding power of a true obsession, of a fixed idea.

During the last months of the year, I decided to leave the Accounting Department, and I presented my resignation. I registered immediately in *Ginásio Santa Mariense*, where I studied until the end of the academic year. And after the exams, I went on to Porto Alegre, ready to fight adversity.

In Porto Alegre, I went to see Walter.

We agreed to live together. And we moved into a garage on rua Fernando Vieira, whose owner let us have it in exchange for violin classes and lessons on elementary school subjects that we gave to his children.

Chapter 22

Our life went by magnificently in the garage, which was partly hidden behind a picturesque avenue of eucalyptus trees.

It was a secluded spot, full of light and shade that the birds enlivened with their resonant joy, lending our abode a poetic and enchanting air.

We often had our meals at an eating-house just across from us on the same street, a favorite of bakers, milkmen, green grocers, and day laborers.

You could kill your hunger there for very little, at any time of day, up until midnight.

The daily specials, and their respective prices, were neatly chalked on a blackboard just outside the place.

The atmosphere wasn't pleasant. All types of people gathered around the small tables covered with stained cloths that delighted the flies. And it was almost always permeated with smoke coming from the kitchen, plus a strong odor of human sweat.

Our meals consisted of a medium-sized coffee with bread and butter in the morning, a blue plate special at mid-day, and the same dish for dinner.

I taught violin. I didn't earn much. But I was satisfied with life because I had lots of time to study.

I read a lot, trying to continually expand my education.

I was suffering from a spiritual anguish that arose as I strove to understand the world. But as I widened my scope of knowledge, I acquired a clearer vision.

Guided by Haeckel, Darwin, Buchner, Comte, Lamarck, Spencer, and other naturalists and philosophers of the last century, I was able, patiently, little by little, to trace the natural origin of the world, and the origins of property, family, and the State.

A rational and scientific interpretation of the causes of cosmic and social phenomena led me across the slow and lengthy evolution of the world, from its primitive and very remote homogeneity to the extraordinary heterogeneity of our day.

I ascertained that everything in the world obeys harmonic and interdependent laws. And that the evolution of nature from extreme simplicity to maximum complexity is one of the characteristic and fundamental traits of progress.

The revelations of Monism, showing me the marvelous unity of the universal whole, brought me profound inner peace.

However, in the realm of sociology, my doubts didn't fade away.

The more that I delved into descriptions of world history and other works, investigating the origin and transformation of society through its different phases, up until the present, the clearer it seemed to me that humanity was following an erroneous path that would never take her, unless she changed direction, to a complete fulfillment of her true and higher purpose, a gradual advance towards perfection.

As a natural consequence of all these discoveries, I felt my belief in God shaken, my belief in the vengeful God of the Bible, the God of a thousand-year-old beard, whose attributes of omniscience, omnipotence, and infinite goodness were not compatible with the objective reality of the world that I lived in. He was a childish God that distributed prizes and punishments without the slightest consideration for equity or justice. For me, the God of Scholastic Theology was reduced to a fistful of laws, eternal and unchangeable, that ruled the world in its pilgrimage across the millennia through time and space, to a destiny that challenged the minds of the sages and the patience of the philosophers, and that successive generations have tried to interpret in their own way to justify the human will to live. . . .

Chapter 23

Almost all Sunday evenings we went out in the company of some friends, also students, to spend a few hours of innocent bohemian pleasure in a peaceful quarter of the city.

We didn't go to nightclubs, nor were we interested in the red-light district.

We started out without any set destination, strolling about at random, just for the pleasure of walking, of finding new streets, drawn by the mirage in the distance. We didn't know yet that all of life's roads always converge at the same point.

Rendenção Park was our favored retreat. There we chose a discreet place where we had long conversations under the trees.

At times, the talks grew too lively, bringing up heated discussions on the most varied subjects and lasting until the early hours of the morning.

Persuaded that discussions, as a rule, bring the light of truth, we tried to provoke them so we could clarify certain doubts, illuminating our minds that were vividly interested in the solutions to all the questions directly related to the well-being of poor humanity.

We couldn't understand why most members of mankind were utterly indifferent to these problems, why they were only concerned with their personal interests, limiting their whole existence, completely, at any price, to the egotistical satisfaction of their own desires, not caring at all about their neighbors, the misfortune of others, or the suffering of their fellow man.

They were, in our eyes, inferior creatures that didn't make any attempt to dignify the species. They lived without knowing why or for what, only attending to their own individual well-being, incapable of foregoing anything, of renouncing anything, or of making any sacrifice. Creatures, in short, that have never felt, burning in their hearts, the sacred flame of a high held ideal, because they have never had a finer vision of human existence. With the true passivity of animals, they only served to thicken the great human herd.

That's how we were then—vibrating with enthusiasm and naïve dreams. . . .

One night, we decided to take a walk through a neighborhood just on the outskirts of the city close to the park.

We were four. Walter, Milton, Bento, and me.

It was a splendid night.

Shimmering in the magnificent blue of the sky, like a divine jewel, among myriads of stars, was the Southern Cross. In the distance, far off, the sinuous line of the hills softly enclosed the horizon. On the other side, sky and ground dissolved into a curtain of shadows. And between earth and sky, something ethereal hovered in the night's sweet warmth. Something that raised our thoughts and desires to the infinite.

We went on silently, rapt in the contemplation of the marvelous spectacle that the night offered us.

"What is it, Walter?" I asked him.

"I don't know. I feel somewhat strange just now. This vast splendor disturbs and saddens me. It makes me think of our measly smallness and the amazing grandeur of the universe. I feel that I would happily sacrifice my own life if it would bring some good to life's disinherited, some benefit to humanity."

"Really," I responded. "The beauty of this nocturnal tableau moves us and makes us think."

And, governed by the same sentiment, we paused mesmerized in front of life's intangible charm.

"Will our life also be so smooth and lovely?" I inquired.

My question, however, died without an answer in the quietude of the night. And we renewed our walk, reaching our destination at a very late hour.

Over this isolated group of homes rested the secret yet expressive sadness of humility. Most were made of wood. Some had a small garden in the front. From one, a drowsy dog, his snout stretched out between his legs, spied us with pricked ears. And, from time to time, a distant bark would disturb the tremendous peace that enveloped that retired quarter, far from the city, that the serene stillness of the night softly cradled.

After walking through a true labyrinth of alleys, we discovered on a corner a small bar.

We went in and took a table.

A tall and robust mulatto with a friendly face and a chef's apron came with a smile to wait on us.

We ordered ranch steaks and beer.

The mulatto spread a cloth over our little table and brought the beer, letting us know with the solicitude of a servant that,

"The steaks won't be long, just a moment or so. . . . ."

And he disappeared into the back.

As we were very thirsty, we began to drink. And the alcohol vapors little by little filled us with a grand lyrical zeal.

Walter began to recite sonnets by the renowned Brazilian Olavo Bilac, his favorite poet. Then it was Milton's turn, and we didn't have to beg him much before he delivered some poems by the popular Portuguese poet, Guerra Junqueiro, while Bento, who had his weekly Saturday algebra quiz the next day, was downcast and sullen because he hadn't yet reviewed the material.

Abruptly, a shout of "by no means!" cut into our fervor.

It was the cook that was bringing us the steaks, protesting,

"By no means," he repeated, speaking to Milton. "It's not right. You, sir, skipped. . . . Two quatrains are missing from the poem you are reciting, sir." Then looking at the group to see what impression his words were making, he added, as he concluded in a pretentious tone, "And I, a humble admirer of the old Lusitanian soothsayer can't let the integrity of that poem be mutilated."

Assuming a superior air, with the steaks in his hands, he began to recite Guerra Junqueiro's "The Blackbird," the entire poem from beginning to end without omitting a word, not even a comma.

This amazing performance left us totally in awe.

"You are a wonder," exclaimed Bento with tremendous admiration.

"Just a poet," corrected the mulatto, swelling with pride.

And he thanked Bento for his praise with an affected bow.

We then asked him if he knew other poets.

"A number of them," the cook replied. "I know the stories of the lives of many of them better than the lives of my most regular customers. Imagine, gentlemen, that I had the patience to teach myself Italian just so that I could read the Divine Comedy in the original."

We looked at each other, incredulous.

But the mulatto pretended not to have noticed anything and went on after a short pause,

"What is more, I also know a bit of prose. I have read a lot. But today life is a bit difficult, and a poor mulatto can't give himself such luxuries. When things were a little more relaxed, I lived glued to the books. I am very fond of the French astronomer Camilo Flammarion. Once, I devoured in only one night his *Plurality of the Planets*. What an extraordinary book, gentlemen. Just fantastic!"

And serving us the steaks, he became serious, adding,

"In the end, what did I get from reading and the *Plurality of the Planets*?"

And with a bitter smile, he concluded,

"After all, you can't fry a planet. . . . "

Chapter 24

The garage became the preferred meeting place for our closest friends, about five, almost all Jewish students or descendants of Jews, that came there for talks whenever their time permitted.

Our conversations almost always revolved around books, authors, and generally transcendent issues. Joined as brothers by an immense and deeply felt desire to educate ourselves, we lived more in the spiritual world of ideas than in the real world of events.

Comfort, luxury, wealth, material pleasures, did not seduce us. We had other aspirations. We were consumed with an enormous yearning to learn, to expand our knowledge, to enrich ourselves with the most beautiful and sublime and with the most essential and eternal that life offers.

We were stirred with incredible excitement each time we made a new conquest in the realm of the intellect, where we were moved and fascinated by the great figures of humanity.

We read a lot. Mostly works on universal themes.

Reading, moreover, delighted us. It was one of our greatest pleasures.

Our eagerness to learn grew stronger and stronger.

We founded a cultural center, with five or six members, and named it The Self-Taught Club, meeting every Sunday, in the afternoon.

Each week we designated one of our members to speak on any subject, of his own choosing.

The inaugural lecture fell to Walter, who spoke on Schopenhauer's concept of happiness, as follows:

"To be happy! A problem as ancient as thought itself.

Dionysism, Stoicism, Christian Asceticism, divergent solutions to the same vital problem. Diverse ways of justifying the human will to be.

Faced with pain man trembles. But love of life is stronger than the fear of suffering. And this can be seen in the illogical reasoning of the theoreticians of Pessimism that never go to the extreme of carrying out the ultimate implications of their arguments.

To suffer seems better than not feeling anything at all, because to suffer is to live. And life, in the end, does not need to be justified; it is worthy for its own sake.

Nonetheless, it is not this that Schopenhauer stated in his introduction to his Aphorisms on the Wisdom of Life.

Yet Schopenhauer lived. He did not sacrifice himself to the rigidity of his metaphysical principles. And in the quiet hours, the philosopher was also a poet. With subtle thoughts, he penetrated the mystery of life. And he discovered the way to be happy. . . .

According to Schopenhauer, an individual's happiness stems from three factors; what he is, what he has and how the world views him.

The first is personality composed of health, beauty, aesthetic sensibilities, intelligence, etc. The other two are external elements, consisting respectively of property and fame, and honor and social position.

But personality is the measure of all bliss. It constitutes, in fact, the substratum of our well-being, the essential element of our happiness.

In the midst of constant transformation, only one's individuality does not change. Essentially, it remains the same. The items in the external world are like the frame of a portrait; they don't alter one's inner structure.

What is outside of ourselves only has the value we give it. We are the source of all values. The world itself is a dead entity that our intelligence coats with significance.

Seeing luxurious objects exhibited for sale, Socrates said: how many things exist that I don't need. And with the suggestion contained in his few words, he added to human wisdom an excellent principle.

So, if it is the Self that determines the importance of the external world, it is clear that our happiness depends most of all on ourselves, on who we are, in the broadest sense.

Among the virtues of personality, health, beauty, and intelligence are invaluable gifts.

From a sound organism, the glory to live is born. From a beautiful body, warm relationships. From intelligence, the honor of self-sufficiency.

In fact, a fertile mind is never alone. The world of ideas, besides being much more fascinating than the world of men, fulfills the needs for social interaction with endless advantages for the individual. That's why we can envy the serenity of the great minds who, absorbed in their dreams, do not seek more than what they have within. Only they reach the highest form of happiness, which corresponds to the highest level of inner riches. And they are the philosophers, the artists, and the saints.

Therefore, we can see that Schopenhauer prefers personal riches to external ones and that he confers the most decisive role in the determination of individual well-being to the riches of the mind.

Every man is trapped in his own personality as if it were a prison that limits the movements of his sensibility or intelligence. The more expansive his prison, the greater the freedom for psychological movements, which is the same as saying the greater the possibilities to feel and to think.

In a blur of gradations, humanity presents an infinite variety of mental types. On one extreme is the inferior man that still suffers greatly the effects of his animal parentage. On the other, the genius, nature's supreme creation.

The former, due to his spiritual void, is constrained to a purely sensual life, seeking all possible pleasures in the external realm. But the genius has within his own individuality the most immediate means to achieve happiness.

With this construct, Schopenhauer also maintains coherence with his metaphysical concept of the world.

For Schopenhauer, it is the will, that irrepressible and blind force that lives deep within all of nature that is the original source of all pain. Man, as part of the fundamental essence of the cosmos, also suffers from the yoke of this eternal and painful power. Any excitement of the will engenders suffering, all the more, the more violent and imperative the desire.

We can counter desire with intelligence, the power of reasoning. Through representation, the mental images and ideas that intelligence produces, man is able to suspend the action of the will. In this way and in this way only, man achieves the metaphysical ideal of a painless life. "In the realm of intelligence pain has no power, all is representation," that is the redemptive truth in Schopenhauer's philosophy.

Philosophy, art, and science are found within the sphere of representation; consequently, they are means to neutralize the action of the will, which results in pleasure that is nothing more than less pain, nothing more than the progressive negation of pain, until reaching absolute repose, the death of the will, nirvana. As the supreme kindler of intelligence, because of the extraordinary force of his creative faculties, the genius is blessed with the power to liberate himself from the will with great consistency. Through representation, he achieves the most perfect ideal of happiness: aesthetic pleasure and philosophical thought.

This is Schopenhauer's concept of happiness from the metaphysical perspective. In practical life, it is called self-sufficiency.

In Schopenhauer's aphorisms there flows the murmur of self-consolation.

Pride in self-sufficient intelligence always flourished in the lives of the great solitary minds. For what isolates men is not space, it is ideas and sensibilities. Numbers are quite inexpressive for those that find in spiritual pleasures sufficient reason for their own existence. Adding figures, which lack souls or sensibilities, has an entirely negative value for these exalted beings.

Indeed, the philosopher explains, formulating the rule of homogeneous affinities: similes simile gaudet. *Like rejoices in like. And without irony, what did Voltaire say? "To a toad, what is beauty . . . ?"*

Bento discussed the origin of man, And I, the origin of music.

But our stay in the garage lasted only a few months.

My family came from Santa Maria, completely ruined, and I went to live with them.

Walter, in turn, moved to a boarding house. The rest of our friends dispersed.

And the Self-Taught Club died away.

Chapter 25

With the coming of my parents to Porto Alegre, we began again the same troubled life of poverty and misery suffered during our earlier years spent in this capital city.

We only had a few hundred mil-reis in savings.[1]

Papa, Solon, and Daniel resolved to try their hands at peddling woolen cloth in the nearby townships.

And that's what they did. With a few pieces of cloth in a bag over their shoulders, they began to develop this type of business.

They mainly worked in farming settlements, away from the township centers. Preferring areas that were far from any stores, they carved out long routes on foot.

But the experience did not match their expectations. The travel costs were considerable. And the profit didn't compensate.

Dissatisfied with the results, they had to look for another way to make a living.

As a bankrupt merchant, Papa had to leave aside certain compunctions. So, not finding any other way to fulfill the family's basic needs, he acquired a wagon and began to buy bottles, cans, and empty sacks. But, since he didn't have the capital for large purchases, he also moved the goods of others.

Solon and Daniel entered the world of credit, sharing their respective profits with a landsman who supplied them with the merchandise they needed, a sort of partnership that was very common among the moneylenders. One of the partners comes in with capital or credit and the other with labor. And the profits are divided on a previously agreed upon basis.

Gradually, everyone adapted to the new life, which is more or less the life that is shared by many families, who, having failed in smaller towns, come to the large urban centers in search of better luck.

And I, after some time of indecision, resolved in spite of everything to continue my studies, counting on the material assistance of my family, who, indeed, never let me down whenever I appealed to them for help, which I only did in cases of extreme necessity.

As I wanted to take the entrance exams, I registered for the preparatory courses.

I duly valued the support my family was giving me and the enormous sacrifice that I was causing them. That's why I sought to thoroughly fulfill the confidence they had deposited in me, by dedicating myself body and soul to my studies.

I didn't leave the house, except on Sunday mornings, when I went to give lessons in Portuguese and arithmetic to a young girl, and on Sunday nights, when I used to stroll through the city with a friend.

I led a life of complete self-denial.

But, as my visits to my student continued, I became enchanted with her charms, until, one day, I fell passionately in love with her.

She was really beautiful.

I still see her, under my eyes, on the virginal purity of the paper on which I am now writing, smiling at me with a smile made of sweetness and light, which fills my soul with sublime radiance and my heart with loving kindness.

I feel, even today, in spite of the elapse of so many years, full of deep-seated emotions, as I call up again her angelical image, her small, fresh mouth, the brilliant ivory of her perfect teeth, the lily-white pureness of her fine skin, almost transparent, the dark gold of her hair which lent her a halo of sainted spirituality, her wide brow, pure and fair, the divine beauty of her marvelous eyes, and the noble delicate lines of her shapely hands.

Her name was. . . . No, I won't mention her name. What significance could it have, on the lips of strangers, the name of a woman that one loved?

None, without a doubt. It would be just a name. Nothing more.

Whereas, for me, it signifies a world of dreams and beauty, where, during a few years, I lived in true ecstasy. Only pronouncing her name, my heart expands with excitement, my soul fills with light, and I feel completely rejuvenated.

Oh, my Lord, only You know how I loved her because it was her saintly beauty that revealed to me Your existence. . . .

In spite of foreseeing that destiny would separate us, as in fact, it did, I still loved her with all the ardor of my youth, with all the purity of my soul, selflessly.

And my platonic sentiments brought me true happiness.

I was satisfied just to see her, to be by her side, to breathe the same air that she breathed, to adore her in silence, deliriously happy in the contemplation of her beauty. And I feel that I would be capable, if life were not to separate us, of spending my whole existence next to her, in this state of heavenly bliss.

I couldn't comprehend life without love, which, for me, is the fundamental reason for our existence. For me, in my misery, seeing my family battle with poverty, Papa buying empty sacks, given up once again to drink, my brothers borrowing in order to sell, love was a necessary refuge, a miraculous shield that could resist the blows of adversity.

It is true that love has been more or less discredited by the coarse and corruptive utilitarianism of our time. But, on the day that man convinces himself that without love there is no salvation, he will reclaim his true place on earth, restoring his ability to redeem himself . . . .

Chapter 26

While taking the preparatory courses, I became an agent in a life insurance company.

I insured the lives of others to keep my own afloat.

Insurance is a good profession. But among other things, to harvest its fruits the agent needs to frequent a circle of the finest, have good social contacts and have the ability to spend freely.

It goes without saying that I lacked all of these.

I began by approaching my own narrow circle.

This done, the doors to any other spheres of action were hermetically shut.

Without any resources and badly dressed, I didn't manage to close on any new policies.

To succeed at climbing the wall that separated me from the field where I hoped to reap positive results, I resorted to a tactic matching the urgency of my situation.

I introduced myself to the director of one of the best secondary schools in Porto Alegre, asking him for a list of the names and addresses of the parents of their students.

To justify my strange request, I confessed that I was a poor student; that I was planning to enter Law School but didn't have the necessary funds. That to obtain them, I had become a life insurance agent. And, as my social contacts were extremely scarce due to my humble position and origin, I had decided that in order to circumvent this difficulty, I would send a letter of introduction, signed by the director of the insurance company, to everyone on the list I was asking for, because it could be presumed that the parents of the students enrolled in this school enjoyed stable economic positions and, therefore, would be able to protect their families with an insurance policy.

The name and address on the envelope and the letter of introduction would lend my communications a stamp of credibility. Thus, the addressees would feel obligated to receive me. And once in the presence of each one of them, it would be relatively easy for me to demonstrate the benefits of having a policy.

The Director listened to me attentively and didn't hesitate to immediately put at my disposal the registration ledger, from which I extracted the list that I wanted.

Yet, my plan didn't bring the expected results. Some of my prospects had moved. Others were incorrectly entered in the ledger. The name of the child appeared in the column for the father and vice versa. This brought me some comically embarrassing moments. For example, I would ask for the person I presumed to be the father, stating that I had a letter for him, and a high school student would come to receive it.

Even so, I wrote various policies, obtaining the needed funds for the entrance exam.

At home, however, the situation grew vastly graver. Business was bad and worsened every day.

We moved to Gloria, just outside Porto Alegre. And, as things didn't improve, we went to live in Teresopolis where we opened a tiny fruit market.

But the market, of which we were almost the exclusive customers, didn't even bring in enough to pay the house rent.

Then Daniel went to Santa Maria where he had the promise of employ-ment. Thoroughly disappointed with life, Papa made a complete and utter surrender to alcohol. And destitution began to encircle our house.

One day we woke up with the market totally empty and without any money. We had arrived at extreme poverty.

What to do?

I thought of the money that I had put aside for the entrance exam. I called to Papa and, showing him how reduced our situation had become, I asked him to abandon his drinking.

I begged. I pleaded. And, to encourage him to start a new life, I put my savings at his complete disposal.

He listened to me with his eyes welling up with tears and his heart torn with pain. Squeezing his hands desperately between his knees, he confessed that my request was more than he could muster. That he was a woeful vic-tim of the damned vice. That he didn't drink for pleasure. That he knew that every chalice he drank had the bitter taste of his wife's tears and those of his beloved sons. That please forgive him. . . . That alcohol had acquired over him the power of a real physical necessity.

Nonetheless, I wasn't discouraged.

I invoked new arguments and ended up saying that I would leave my studies for a year to help him in his moral rehabilitation if he promised, under oath, not to drink anymore.

Tears rolled down his cheeks where misfortune had carved out fur-rowed hollows. Gradually, he too became infected with the optimism I expressed, as I tried to persuade him that he could still turn himself into a man equal to others. Finally, in front of the whole family, he accepted a solemn commitment not to return to drink. Deeply touched, I felt his poor thankful soul in the handshake he gave me to seal our pact.

It is impossible to describe our happiness. For the first time, we cried with gladness.

A new dawn was breaking in the somber sky that covered our lives.

That same day, we settled on our plan to move closer to the center of the city. And, that weekend, we rented a house on rua Lobo da Costa, where we went to live.

With the money that I gave him, Papa became a bric-a-brac peddler.

To see him go out every morning, bent over and beaten down by life's reverses, carrying his odds and ends, my heart bled from both pity and pain.

Fueled by the best intentions, he had exchanged trade for agriculture, emigrating to the New World. He had left his native land, his mother, his relatives, and friends to become a farmer here in Brazil. How many hopes did he nurture during the ocean crossing? How many happy dreams did he cradle during the course of the voyage? And now there he was broken down, gray-haired, and mistreated by life, offering knickknacks door to door like a beggar.

A year went by.

But luck did not smile on us in rua Lobo da Costa.

Papa fell ill. He went through two operations. One for appendicitis and the other for a strangled hernia.

No matter how much we fought, everything always went wrong.

Following Daniel's example, Solon also left for a city in the interior of the state, where a spring had appeared. Considered miraculous, it attracted large pilgrimages of sufferers, disillusioned by medical science, in hopes, of short duration, of recovering their health in those waters, whose therapeutic properties seemed to have been overly praised.

Then, to save funds, the rest of us moved to a cottage on rua Francisco Ferrer, the same street where I lived when I came to Porto Alegre to take my first exams.

Shortly thereafter, Solon sent a letter, inviting Papa to join him in the city near the spring, where, Solon said, Papa would find it easy to sell his wares.

Papa accepted the invitation, going there with the family. He promised to send me the money needed for the university entrance exam I was preparing for.

Chapter 27

With my parents' move to the interior of the state, I remained alone in the house with our dog and cat, without anything to feed them with and without a cent in my pockets. But being more or less accustomed to a lack of money, which was, you could say, my habitual state, I didn't let myself worry too much about these new circumstances, trusting destiny to find the solution to the difficulties that could by chance arise. On the contrary, I was quite pleased with the absence of my family because I foresaw a fortunate occurrence, a truly providential opportunity to prepare for my entrance exam in an atmosphere of seclusion and solitude, full of silence and tranquility.

But I had totally forgotten about Pilot and Mimi, who weren't at all happy with the new situation and immediately began to demand food. Especially Mimi, whose meows became unbearable.

I thought the animals' complaints were reasonable and I sought a way to satisfy them.

I remembered the store, *Armazem Pasqual*, that was near our house, where I had a little bit of credit since the first time I came to Porto Alegre because I used to make my student purchases there, paying my debts relatively promptly.

I went to that store and bought, on account, bread, salami, and oranges.

I returned and gave out the salami in equal parts to the dog and the cat, while I ate the bread with the oranges.

Then, I made the bed, swept the house, and, after putting everything in order I began to study the essential points of philosophy, psychology, and logic, subjects that without a doubt are very interesting when the stomach is full.

We were in the month of February, in the middle of summer, a terrible summer, scorching.

It was like an oven inside the small, low cottage, covered with sheets of zinc. The heat was unbearable, suffocating us even with the door and windows open.

But, concerned with my studies, I lived indifferent to the world that surrounded me.

At midday and again at the dinner hour I made the same purchases. Once again, I divided the salami between my companions, and I remained with the bread and the oranges.

It was my breakfast, lunch, and dinner.

But at mealtimes I would strike the silverware on thoroughly empty plates in order not to expose myself to the neighbors who from natural curiosity had begun to peer into the life of misery that I led. To give them the impression that I was regularly ordering in cooked food, I pretended to eat soup and cut imaginary steaks.

Then, to complete the illusion and remove any disbelief, I washed, loudly, the clean dishes. . . .

This done, I returned to my worktable and bent over my books, sweaty and famished, trying to understand, through scholastic dialectics, the concept of infinite divine goodness.

I am convinced that hunger is unable to discern this theological dogma.

But the dog and the cat, who couldn't live from illusions, didn't leave me in peace. They were not satisfied with the rations of salami I gave them. They were always hungry, always asking and sniffing for food.

They wouldn't let me be. So, I made superhuman efforts to remain deaf to their moaning.

However, in one of those rare and lamentable coincidences when destiny seems to take delight in human suffering, Mimi, on one of the first nights of our life of misery, gave birth to five kittens, whose meows, resembling the cries of infants, left me desperate, almost crazed.

This inopportune increase to the family seriously aggravated our life together.

I was worried, troubled, nervous, thinking of a way to dispose of the newborn family members, creatures too weak to compete with us in our starvation contest.

That night, I settled them in an empty kerosene can and displayed them on the sidewalk in the hope that they would be picked up by some merciful soul. But, either because no one walked by there that night or because the hearts that could feel for the misery of others didn't have anything they could give to these hungry ones, these poor fellows that had the misfortune to be born in the house of a poor student screamed so much that late that night I didn't have any other choice than to get up and bring them in. But since they continued meowing without stopping, I took an extreme decision.

I got dressed. I shut Mimi in a room, threw the kittens in the bottom of a sack and carried them to rua da Independencia where I left them in the doorway of the first well-to-do house.

It was the first, and that I can remember, until today, the only evil action I took during my lifetime.

Mimi looked for the kittens all that night and during the next day, filling the house with her anguished and piercing desperate-mother wailing.

Robbed of the objects of her maternal love and beset by hunger, she abandoned me a few days later, securing another master. Pilot, on the other hand, didn't want to betray the proverbial loyalty of his species. He stayed with me, enduring hunger heroically.

He lay down next to my study table, and he stared at me at length with tender looks, pleading. At times, he got up and timidly rested his paw on my legs, petting me. I tried to appear untouched by his fondling. But it touched the depths of my heart. I felt so sorry for him. I could no longer stand his sweet, resigned gaze. It made me suffer terribly. And I resolved to also free myself from him.

One morning I called him, and we went out. Assuming, naturally, that I was going to the store to make my usual purchases, he accompanied me, happily, with a lifted tail and pricked ears.

He set out running in front of me and at a certain distance he abruptly stopped, turned around, and returned right away in an out of control sprint, jumping over me, crazy with glee.

Yet, when he saw me head off in another direction, he completely lost his joy, as if he had read my mind. He followed me with little enthusiasm, with his tail between his legs and his ears limp, revealing, in his expressive look, a kind of premonition of what I intended to do.

I turned the corner on to rua da Independencia heading, on foot, to the center of the city, where I planned to free myself of the dog, leaving him lost among the crowd of passers-by and then return home immediately, taking another route, entirely different from the one I took with him.

Since it was the first time that I took him to the city's center, I was sure he would not find the way to return home.

While I was walking, thinking about executing this perverse plan, Pilot was following me, half-heartedly, suspicious.

The sun glowed with all its splendor, in a cloudless sky, radiating a vivid, metallic, fiery light.

Dazzling reflections sparkled on the tracks of the tramway, on the polished stones of the street, and on the panes of the windows.

There was a true orgy of light everywhere.

Arriving at the end of Independencia, I went down rua da Praia.

Pilot didn't leave off. He followed me closely, sniffing my steps.

In places where the movement of people was more intense, he stuck by my feet.

I soon realized that any attempt at escape would be frustrated.

After taking him for various turns on that street, I stopped, nonchalantly in front of the old Café Colombo. And there I stayed until, evading his watch, I managed to quickly enter the café, without him seeing me, exiting right away onto rua General Camara, by a back door, which I closed. Then, with quickened steps, nervous, dismayed, distressed as if I had committed some crime, I reached the corner of rua Sete de Setembro. I stopped for a few moments, looked behind me and all around, and didn't see him.

I was free, finally free.

I turned the corner, relieved, and returned home by another route.

I spent the rest of the morning and a large part of the afternoon alone, full of remorse for what I had done. Nothing could console me, not even thinking that someone would surely take him in, giving him a better life than he had led with me.

I wandered around the different rooms of the house, upset, thinking of Pilot. No matter how hard I tried to forget him, I couldn't. My conscience attacked me, not leaving me be. The memory of having abandoned a poor famished dog, in the sea of human indifference, troubled me greatly.

Suddenly I hear a noise at the door.

I shuddered, scared. And moved by a strange premonition of fear and delight, I opened the door cautiously.

It was Pilot.

Pilot! I exclaimed, overjoyed, holding out my arms to him.

He jumped up on me. Greatly moved, I hugged him close, while he covered me with gulping kisses. And I felt, in these expressions of affection, all his forgiveness for what I had done to him.

Only dogs know how to forgive unconditionally. . . .

We went on living as good friends, enduring hunger together. But, as the days passed, I began to have some sharp twinges in my back, frequent headaches, and constant fatigue. Next, I was overcome by a total physical weakness that knocked me out.

I decided to find a boarding house that also offered carry-out meals, and I convinced the owner, to whom I divulged my precarious situation, to provide food for me and for Pilot until my parents' return.

Pilot wins the prize for this test of our ability to resist hunger. But after Mahatma Gandhi and other idealists started to participate in this type of contest, the canine class was completely demoralized, and the honor passed to the human species. . . .

Afterword

When the colorful brochures offering agricultural life in Brazil reached Zagradowka in the early twentieth century, Marcos Iolovitch's father, Yossef, was a Jewish shopkeeper in this small Ukrainian village one hundred and seventy miles northeast of Odessa in the southern Ukrainian province of Kherson. Yossef's life was gliding "along placidly, always maintaining the same rhythm, without any bumps in the road".[1]

The Jews in Kherson province "were among the wealthiest and most stable in the Pale of Settlement [the Western Russian area where Jews were allowed to reside]." They followed fewer traditional Jewish practices and enjoyed much higher levels of education than Jews in neighboring provinces. By 1897, 45.1 percent of the Jewish men and 24.6 percent of the Jewish women in the province were able to read Russian.[2] But Yossef dreamed of emigrating to Brazil, to the agricultural colony of Quatro Irmãos, to become a farmer and to pass on to his sons the peaceful harmony of agricultural life.[3]

Dreams of turning Jewish tradesmen into farmers were not new. Efforts date back to the early nineteenth century and feature some strange bedfellows, including Czars, wealthy Jewish railroad tycoons and even the Mennonites. Like Thomas Jefferson many late eighteenth century and early nineteenth-century thinkers believed that "cultivators of the earth are the most valuable citizen. . . , the most vigorous . . . [and] the most virtuous. . ." .[4] Russian Czar Alexander I was in agreement.

Upon his rise to the throne in 1801 Czar Alexander I faced a dual dilemma. First, how could he populate the "desolate steppes" of southern Ukraine that Russia had recently annexed from the Ottomans following the Russo-Turkish Wars?[5] In addition, how could he integrate the close to one million Jews who had recently come under Russian rule through the acts of partition that divided the lands of the Polish-Lithuanian Commonwealth among Prussia, Austria and Russia?[6]

Believing that the wealth of nations depended on agriculture[7] and that as farmers Jews would be less "parasitical"[8] he passed a law in 1804 allowing Jews to purchase land and settled tens of thousands of these Jews in thirty-eight agricultural colonies in the southern Ukrainian provinces of Kherson and Yekaterinoslav.[9] When the crops did not totally fulfill their promise, the Russian government enlisted Mennonite farmers in the "convert the Jews into farmers movement." The government paid Mennonites to live as "model farmers" in the Jewish agricultural colonies and to teach in their schools.[10] Though not always successful, by 1900 close to 42,000 Jews[11] were living in these farming communities and those living in "twenty-two colonies had achieved standards of living equal to or better than those of their non-Jewish neighbors".[12] In fact, the father of Lev Bronstein, better known as Leon Trotsky, was a successful Jewish farmer in Kherson province.

German Mennonites had been settling in Ukraine since the eighteenth century, when their compatriot, Czarina Catherine the Great, offered them religious freedom and financial incentives. By 1911, 104,000 Mennonites were farming on their own lands in southern Ukraine.[13] Zagradowka, Yossef's village, abutted sixteen Mennonite farming colonies spread across 60,000 acres[14] and Mennonite farmers were very likely customers in Yossef's store.

These Mennonite farms and the Jewish agricultural colonies that were located only six miles from the city of Krivoy Rog, which Yossef visited regularly to purchase his merchandise, most certainly fanned his passion for agriculture. Like Jefferson, he came to believe that farming was the "cleanest and most honorable of professions".[15]

But Yossef knew he could never become a farmer in Russia. Russian laws had changed, and Jews could no longer buy land.[16] Some restraints on land purchases were issued in the 1860s but in 1882, following the assassination of the liberal serf-freeing Czar Alexander II, a crime often blamed on the Jews, the Russian government passed laws that severely curtailed the rights of Jews to purchase land. They also severely affected all their economic activities and educational opportunities.[17] So Yossef must have truly felt that his dreams had come true when emigration recruitment brochures reached Zagradowka on that clear April morning, with colorful depictions of southern Brazilian wheat fields mirroring the crops that surrounded him in Kherson province.

Another powerful actor in the "turn the outcast Jew into a productive citizen through farming effort" would enable Yossef to realize this dream. This benefactor was Baron Maurice de Hirsch, a German-born Belgian financier who had made the bulk of his fortune building the Vienna-Constantinople railroad.[18]

Following the passing of the restrictive laws in the 1880s, the socio-economic state of Russian Jews deteriorated rapidly.[19] Many wealthy Western European Jews became deeply concerned. Baron Hirsch was the most active among them.

Baron Hirsch saw agriculture as the solution. He had an almost "compulsive feeling" that Jews should become farmers, that agriculture was the road away from misery.[20] Hirsch saw no reason why Russian and other Eastern European Jews could not become farmers. The relative success of the Jewish farming colonies in Ukraine had not overcome what Hirsch called the "typical reproach" that Jews were not suited for farming. So he asked that doubters look at history. He reminded them that in Christ's time the Jews were the farmers, while commerce was conducted by "Phoenicians, Greeks and [other] Mediterranean peoples".[21]

At first Baron Hirsch hoped to realize this transformation "in-place" within Russia itself. He offered the Russian government fifty million francs (approximately $US 245 million in today's dollars) to allow him to educate the Jews through "the establishment of elementary and agricultural schools." But despite spending today's equivalent of $US5 million in bribes, the Baron's negotiations with the Russian government did not succeed, which " . . . convinced [him] that emigration was the only solution for the Russian Jews".[22]

At about the same time, in 1889, Baron Hirsch learned by chance of 500 Russian Jewish immigrants existing only on crackers and housed in railroad wagons in rural Argentina. The land they had been promised previous to emigration was not available upon their arrival.[23] The Baron stepped in to set them up as farmers. Seeing an actualization of his dream for Russian Jews inspired Hirsch to dedicate significant resources to settling more impoverished Jews in the New World. He decided "to stake my wealth and intellectual powers . . . to give a portion of my companions in faith the possibility of finding a new existence, primarily as farmers and also as handicraftsman, in those lands where the laws and religious tolerance permit them to carry on the struggle for existence".[24]

In 1891, as memoriam to his only son, Baron Hirsch formed the Jewish Colonization Agency (JCA) with working capital of two million pounds sterling (equivalent of $US250 million in today's dollars) "to assist and promote the emigration of Jews from any part of Europe or Asia . . . and to form and establish colonies in various parts of North and South America . . . ".[25] The JCA Board consisted of Lord Rothschild and many of the "grand dukes of British and French Jewry",[26] but Baron Hirsch contributed 99 percent of the funding.[27] Rothschild was spending most of his money developing Palestine.

At first, the JCA focused on settling Jews in scarcely populated Argentina with its vast low-cost fertile plains. By 1906 there were close to 7,000 settlers living in JCA-supported Argentine farming colonies.[28]

The JCA and its sister organization the Baron de Hirsch Fund also carried out settlement plans in Canada and the United States. While I was conducting research for this afterword, an old friend pointed out that the chicken farm in Connecticut that I visited each summer while growing up began as a Baron Hirsch project.[29] Like Marcos' family in Zagradowka who benefitted from the prosperity of the gentleman with whom his grandmother "had entered into a second marriage three years after the death of her first husband",[30] my childhood excursions were thanks to the gentleman with whom my grandmother had entered into a second marriage three years after the death of her first husband.

The chicken farm was his childhood home, part of Baron Hirsch's project in Colchester, Connecticut. The Colchester settlers, like those in Argentina, were successful. In Colchester, the colonists specialized in easily marketable products, chickens, eggs, and milk, that they could sell to nearby metropolitan areas. They also offered inexpensive kosher bed and breakfast inns, as retreats for residents of New York's lower East Side and other urban Jewish immigrant neighborhoods.[31]

In 1896 Baron Hirsch passed away, bequeathing seven million pounds sterling (equivalent to $US 1.12 billion in today's dollars) to the JCA.[32] A newly elected board of trustees voted to use some of this windfall to expand JCA's colonization activities to Brazil,[33] where the JCA purchased land in 1902.[34] But in Brazil, success would prove to be more difficult.

In October 1904 the first homesteaders reached Philippson, JCA's initial colony in Brazil, and the birthplace of Marcos Iolovitch's wife.[35] The JCA had not yet built the houses they had promised, so the thirty-seven families were housed in barracks. It took months for the settlers to be assigned land and, once assigned, they discovered it was very hard to farm.

Unlike the Argentine colonies on the flat pampas, Philippson was located in a hilly region that is really more suitable for grazing than farming. But, with difficulty, it could be farmed, if you knew how. The great majority of these settlers, however, had no farming experience. Then there were the droughts, locusts, and even typhoid fever.[36]

It must have seemed hopeless, as confirmed by a French student, Pierre Denis, who visited both Philippson and the Argentine JCA colonies in 1910. Denis, who later became de Gaulle's finance minister during World War II,[37] wrote "the success of this venture [Philippson] has not been remarkable and

... will probably remain an isolated experiment. In Argentina the Jewish col-onies have multiplied and are very numerous and the Jews form an important element of the agricultural population, but there is no reason to believe that they will ever hold a like position in Rio Grande".[38]

JCA did take some measures to improve conditions in Philippson. In 1908, the JCA staff established a dairy as another source of income. To address the children's educational needs, a teacher from France was sent to Lisbon to learn Portuguese before coming to Philippson. But these improvements were too late.

The settlers had discovered that there were urban centers in Rio Grande do Sul where life was easier, both elementary and high schools were available, and livelihoods could be made through commerce. By 1909 the majority had left Philippson[39] with most settling in the city of Santa Maria, only nine miles away, or Porto Alegre, almost 200 hundred miles distant. In that same year, Porto Alegre's first minion was held (the quorum of ten men necessary for Jewish prayer sessions to be held).[40]

So did the JCA retreat south to Argentina? No. Instead, in 1909 they bought land for a much larger Brazilian colony a little further north in Rio Grande. Philippson was built on a twenty-two square mile tract of land. The new colony, Quatro Irmãos, where the Iolovitch family would settle, con-sisted of 362 square miles. Why this massive expansion after Philippson's lackluster success? Could it be that converting Russian Jews into successful farmers was not the principal goal of these Brazilian colonies?

Baron Hirsch was not the only Belgian to make a fortune in railroads. In the late nineteenth and early twentieth century the Belgian financial community was underwriting the development and expansion of railroads all over the world.[41] The Philippson colony was named for Franz Philippson, a Belgian banker and president of the Brussels Jewish community who had built the railroads in the Belgian Congo and was the president and owner of the *Compaigne Auxiliaire de Chemins du Fer au Bresil*.

In 1898 the *Compaigne Auxiliaire* won a major contract to build and maintain railroads in Rio Grande do Sul and opened an office in Santa Maria, just fourteen kilometers from the site of the future Philippson colony.[42] By 1902 *Compaigne Auxiliaire* controlled most of the railroads in the state[43] and, by 1905, controlled all of them and held the contract for the completion of the railroad grid.[44] Quatro Irmãos was to be located just nineteen kilometers from the main railroad line. This line would eventually connect Rio de Janeiro and São Paulo with Montevideo, Uruguay.

These business interests were key factors in the JCA Board's decision to expand into Brazil and to open a second colony even when the first one was failing. This new board was not quite as fervent as Baron Hirsch in its desire to assist Jewish immigrants.[45] But in Rio Grande they saw a confluence of business and charitable interests.[46] Staying within the by-laws that required the JCA to "assist and promote Jewish emigration",[47] the Board realized they could use JCA funds to open immigrant-farming colonies near the Brazilian railroad lines. These colonies would satisfy the stipulation in all government contracts that "obliged all foreign railroad construction companies within 15 years [of signing a contract] to settle along the railroads they built one thousand native or immigrant farmers . . . ".[48] In addition, settling immigrants would reap *Compaigne Auxiliaire* the generous financial incentives the Brazilian federal government was offering railroad companies for settling foreign immigrants, "$200 for each house constructed . . . ; $100 [per family] when the family has been settled for six months; $200 [per family] when . . . settled for a year. . . ; $5,000 for each group of 50 rural lots occupied by families . . . ".[49]

Next, the JCA Board saw commercialization of timber as one of the colonies' principal goals.[50] The railroad lines were being built through vast forests of pines and cedars that could supply substantial profits, as lumber was in high demand in nearby Argentina.[51] In fact, the colonists were forbidden to deforest their plots without JCA approval.

Quatro Irmãos had 50,000 hectares of forest.[52] So, in a commercial context the expansion to this new colony makes good sense. It also explains why the JCA did not bother to supply competent agricultural advisors.

In Philippson immigrants at least had barracks to live in. Iolovitch relates how, when his family arrived in Quatro Irmãos, there weren't even barracks available. His family was housed on the homesteads of earlier immigrants until the barracks for the new immigrants were built. Then his family waited months for their homestead to be assigned.[53] In fact, just as the Iolovitch family was arriving in Quatro Irmãos, the colony's administrators were asking JCA in Paris to cease or at least minimize new immigration, as the colony could not handle any more.[54]

But even with their own homestead, Yossef and his sons were never able to become successful farmers. Their three-year stay in Quatro Irmãos was a time of suffering, horrific, sometimes fatal, accidents, and, ultimately, hunger. As Iolovitch writes, "we didn't know how to tame our cattle or how to prepare the land".[55] Of course they didn't and, again, there was no one to help them. The gentleman sent to administer Quatro Irmãos, Mr. Rosenberg, knew nothing of farming, a fact readily admitted in JCA correspondence.[56] And, for many years, there was no resident agricultural expert in Quatro Irmãos. There was only Mr. Tisserand, the agricultural counselor at the JCA office in Paris to whom questions could be sent. I imagine that by the time the answers arrived the planting season would have been over. In any event, Mr. Tisserand thought that the Quatro Irmãos soil was only good for planting cassava and peanuts,[57] not the golden crop of wheat promised in the JCA recruitment brochures that so excited Iolovitch's father back in Zagradowka.

By 1915, three years after Quatro Irmãos' founding, only one-third of the original settlers remained.[58] The others had moved to the cities. In 1916 Iolovitch's family took the same route and left for Porto Alegre. Iolovitch writes that he didn't know how or from where "Papa managed to get the money for the trip".[59] It might have been from the colony's administrators themselves. In response to the reports of serious problems in Quatro Irmãos, JCA Paris suggested as one solution helping the immigrants leave the colony and seek work in the cities.[60] But before they could leave the colony, hunger forced Iolovitch's father and older brothers to go out as day laborers, helping to build a railroad. And that is exactly what the JCA administrators of Quatro Irmãos wanted. To transport the wood, a branch line was needed. Have the immigrants build it was the directive from JCA, Paris.[61]

When the Iolovitch family reached Porto Alegre in 1916, they found a modern city of 150,000,[62] complete with electric streetcars, theaters, cafes, and cinemas. Beautiful squares with elegant theaters and government buildings graced the town. Education and progress were the city's priorities. Porto Alegre boasted university-level medical, engineering, and law schools and an important public library. Electric plants powered large metalworking and paper producing factories. It was a city with a level of political, economic, and intellectual activity way beyond its size, a city extensively populated by European immigrants or their descendants.[63]

European immigration to the southern border province of Rio Grande do Sul, 700 miles distant from the capital in Rio de Janeiro, began in 1742 when Porto Alegre, Brazil's southernmost state capital, was founded by sixty Portuguese couples from the Azores. Many more followed. By 1775 Azoreans made up 55 percent of Rio Grande's population.[64]

The Azoreans landed in a territory a little larger than the size of New York State and Pennsylvania combined. When they arrived, the province was inhabited by only 5,000 souls, mainly ranchers, *gauchos* or cowboys and *bandeirantes* or bandits, who were interested in finding gold and enslaving the few remaining indigenous inhabitants.

The lands that comprise Rio Grande were given to Spain in 1506 under the Papal Line of Demarcation that divided the world between Spain and

Portugal.[65] The Spanish were never greatly interested in this territory. It was principally the Jesuits and their missions that populated Rio Grande until the late seventeenth century in an area not too far from the location of the twentieth-century JCA colonies.

The Jesuits introduced cattle in the 1620s.[66] Cattle raising prospered and grew to become the basis of the territory's chief economic activity and even today still produces 10 percent of the state's exports.[67] Americans and Europeans who enjoy Brazilian *rodizio* steak houses with their rotating skewers of meat carved at your table owe these Jesuits a mighty thank you. This *rodizio* tradition hails directly from Rio Grande.

In 1676 the Vatican turned its favor toward the Portuguese, assigning Rio Grande to the Diocese of Rio de Janeiro.[68] The Portuguese grabbed the opportunity and started settlements. The Spanish were not pleased, and many small wars resulted. But the Portuguese finally won control of Rio Grande do Sul and sent the Azoreans to Rio Grande to form permanent Portuguese settlements so that the Spanish would never come back.

In the 1820s the now independent Brazilian monarchy, still a little concerned about Spanish forays in the south and seeing a chance to tap unemployed veterans of the Napoleonic Wars, offered subsidies to "hard-working" Germans to settle as farmers in Rio Grande.[69] In the 1830s the subsidies stopped, and immigration was further interrupted by a ten-year war, an effort to gain Rio Grande's independence from Brazil. The attempt failed even though the Italian hero Giuseppe Garibaldi led many of the local fighters, but the Gauchos never gave up their desire for political control, as we shall see.[70]

After the war the central government in Rio decided that the states should handle immigration. The wealthy cattle-raising Gaucho leaders, believing that the Brazilian-born "plebeians" were too lazy to clear the land and develop successful farms, responded by offering subsidies to German immigrants and later to Italians as well, although official support for this assistance often waivered throughout the nineteenth century.[71] Perhaps that is one of the reasons that foreign railroad companies eventually ended up with the responsibility for this support.

The Brazilians also realized that freedom of religion was important for both attracting and keeping immigrants. In 1881 the Brazilian government granted voting rights to non-Catholics. Full freedom of religion, which fulfilled Baron Hirsch's stipulation that the JCA only settle immigrants in "those lands where the laws and religious tolerance permit them to carry on the struggle for existence"[72] came a decade later. This guarantee was included in the both the federal and Rio Grande state constitutions of 1891.

These documents were promulgated after the Gaucho General, Deodoro da Fonseca, successfully led a military coup against the Brazilian monarch and became the first elected president of the new Brazilian Republic. Perhaps he reasoned that if Rio Grande do Sul could not be free of Brazilian control then Rio Grande would control Brazil.

Though not as generous as they might have been, Rio Grande's pro-immigrant policies worked. By 1933 when Iolovitch was twenty-seven, out of a total population of 2.7 million, there were 500,000 people of German descent in the state and 300,000 of Italian descent along with many Poles, Jews and Lebanese.[73] And once the anti-German emotions of the WWI period subsided, the immigrants formed a society of mutual respect. In the 1930s the anniversary of the Germans' first landing in Rio Grande in 1824 was even celebrated as an official State holiday.[74] Today close to 90 percent of Porto Alegre's citizens have European ancestry. Jews comprise a higher percentage of Porto Alegre than the corresponding figures for Jews in either the city of São Paulo or the city of Rio de Janeiro.[75]

The state's temperate climate and its European-like landscape probably pleased the immigrants. Rio Grande's continued strong support for the separation of church and state must have also been a comfort to the Jews as well as the Protestant Germans. For example, in 1920 the state's congressional delegation went so far as to oppose a federal bill to constitute December 25 a national holiday[76] and in 1925 opposed a constitutional amendment that would have united the Catholic Church with the Federal government[77].

The immigrants formed a prosperous, family-oriented society. It became "Brazil's most middle-class state capital".[78] Ostentation was absent, even when the prosperity of some families reached notable heights. An American businessman, residing in the city in 1931, explained that the Depression had brought few bankruptcies to Rio Grande (as compared with the many in São Paulo) because "the buying market is sound and conservative. They will not buy more than they can afford".[79] Even in the 1990s when I lived in Porto Alegre there were few restaurants and the movie theaters had few patrons. Entertainment was still found quietly at home.

The prosperity was sustained by the sound "self-supporting" industries that the immigrants developed.[80] In 1923 the American Consul warned the State Department that there was "not the opportunity here for American trade as there is manufacturing to supply all local needs".[81] That manufacturing now supplies the world. For example, almost all of the Brazilian shoes and wine exported to the US and Europe originate in Rio Grande do Sul, the products of German and Italian immigrant entrepreneurs. And it was the Gauchos that made sure the goods could be transported. German immigrants in Porto Alegre founded VARIG, Brazil's first major airline. The acronym stands for Rio Grandense Airlines.

However, the Germans had been settling in Rio Grande do Sul since 1824 and the Italians since 1875. A few German Jews reached Rio Grande in the second half of the nineteenth century, but the first major influx of Jews began with the opening of the Philippson colony in 1904. So, by the period described in *On a Clear April Morning*, approximately 1913–1930, Jews had only been in the state for a few years. They had not yet had time to construct the financial footholds that would allow them to ride out, or take advantage of, the tumultuous times those years encompassed.

"During World War I Brazil suffered inflation, shortages and capital market shifts. . . ."[82] But in Rio Grande there were other economic upheavals as well. Throughout the war, in Porto Alegre, where those of German descent owned many of the businesses, thousands marched in anti-German demonstrations. And these businesses became the targets when the demonstrations turned violent. In fact, shortly after the Iolovitch family reached Porto Alegre, the worst anti-German violence occurred. On April 15 and 16, 1917, right after Brazil broke off relations with Germany, following the sinking of a Brazilian ship, rioters in Porto Alegre burned and looted stores. They also burned a complete city block to the ground and shot up streetcars, seriously wounding passengers. Violent demonstrations followed in other Rio Grande do Sul locations with large German populations.[83]

In the 1920s the Brazilian hero Luis Carlos Prestes, affectionately called the "Knight of Hope," began his 15,000 mile, two and a half year "Prestes' Column" march across the country with revolts in Rio Grande do Sul. Though Prestes fought in the name of transparent, honest government and equal treatment for all, these violent uprisings brought chaos to many and even caused most of the surviving colonists in Philippson and Quatro Irmãos to join those who had earlier moved to the cities.[84]

Economically, the revolts were a disaster. They disrupted business and caused urban unemployment. Rail service was continually interrupted so goods and fuel often did not reach the interior of the state and sometimes didn't even reach Porto Alegre. These shortages brought inflation and greatly heightened the cost of living.[85]

In the interior of the state, near the fighting, residents, including Jews, were robbed, beaten, kidnapped, and even murdered. Santa Maria, the city the Iolovitch family moved to after a few years in Porto Alegre and where one of the first synagogues in Rio Grande do Sul was built in 1923, saw so much fighting that residents literally had to barricade themselves in their homes.[86] Could some of this fighting have resulted in the fire that burned a neighbor's shop and brought looting to the Iolovitch store, driving Iolovitch's father to drink again? Perhaps, but in any case, this was not a time or place for those starting with nothing to amass the funds to join the ranks of the wealthy.

That is what Iolovitch's father and many other Jews discovered. They didn't know the language, or the customs, and times were tough. As Iolovitch relates, they chose first to earn their living as peddlers because this occupation "didn't demand much capital nor knowledge of the language".[87] With high unemployment it makes sense that many customers didn't even have the funds for these peddlers' inexpensive goods. Not a problem, these creative businessmen sold on the installment plan with the credit records carried in their heads.[88] Once some capital was raised, they opened small shops selling clothes and a general line of goods. But real wealth wouldn't begin to come to the Jews of Rio Grande do Sul until the effects of the world-wide Depression and another series of politically motivated skirmishes centered in the state had subsided.

Iolovitch writes of the early years when survival could be literally hand to mouth. That was probably why he first called this story of immigration *The Disinherited*. The Iolovitch family had left a modest, but comfortable existence in Zagradowka for what, they asked themselves, as death, poverty, and alcoholism plagued them.

But like Iolovitch, whether prosperous or struggling, the immigrants in Rio Grande do Sul read. Between 1885 and 1916, 163 journals and magazines were founded in Porto Alegre. Newspaper circulation in that era was as high as in much more populous Rio de Janeiro or São Paulo.[89] Bookstores with works both in Portuguese and German flourished. Rio Grande has led Brazil in literacy since 1890. By 1920, the level had reached 39 percent in the state compared to 30 percent in São Paulo and a national average of 25 percent.[90] In fact, Porto Alegre is sometimes called The City of the Books. The annual book fair, now in its sixty-fifth year, attracts over 1.3 million visitors.[91]

Porto Alegre's climate of intellectual inquiry nurtured Iolovitch. In *On a Clear April Morning* he describes the endless discussions in the garage he inhabited as a student that "almost always revolved around important books, authors and the fundamental issues of life".[92] I imagine that it was in the bookstore Livraria do Globo that many of these books were purchased or perhaps even read when funds were short. And it was Livraria do Globo, and its support for new writers, that gave Iolovitch the chance to become a published author.

The Livraria de Globo, founded in Porto Alegre in 1883 was a meeting place for intellectuals, politicians and anyone interested in books and ideas.[93] It also had a branch in Santa Maria, where Iolovitch and his family lived for many years. The Livraria not only sold the best translations and Brazilian authors. It also produced them.

Editora do Livraria Globo became one of the finest publishing houses in Brazil producing works by new North American, European and Brazilian writers. Its staff included many immigrants, Jews, Germans, Italians, a real multi-cultural intellectual petri dish.[94] Globo's translations were the best in the country, publishing translations of Marcel Proust, Virginia Woolf, Thomas Mann, James Joyce, and many more world-famous greats. In 1933, for example, Globo published the first Portuguese version of Aldous Huxley's *Point Counter Point*.

The intellectual spirit and energy behind Editora Globo was Iolovitch's good friend, Erico Verissimo who served as Globo's Literary Director and who went on to become one of Brazil's best-known writers. He spent many years in the United States, where his successful career continued. In the 1940s and 50s Macmillan published eight of his books, and in 1957 his novel *Night* was dramatized on nation-wide television starring Jason Robards and E.G. Marshall.[95]

Globo also published an important cultural magazine which featured exclusive interviews with Neruda and Sartre and where articles by Iolovitch shared pages with Ortega y Gasset, George Bernard Shaw, and Luigi Pirandello.[96]

In 1932 Livraria do Globo published Iolovitch's first book *Eu e tu* (I and Thou), a group of poems. In 1940 Globo published *Numa Clara Manha de Abril* with Verissimo himself convincing Iolovitch to change the title from the *Disinherited* to *On a Clear April Morning*. Iolovitch's only other book, *Preces Profanas* (Secular Prayers) was also published by Globo in 1949.

Today Baron Hirsch's colonies in North and South America are closed although a few immigrants did remain on the land. The descendants of the immigrants Hirsch sponsored are spread throughout the world as respected businesspeople, professionals, and artists.

In Brazil, the Philippson and Quatro Irmãos colonies failed but the immigrants didn't. Their successes allowed them to fulfill Baron Hirsh's wish "to give a portion of my companions in faith the possibility of finding a new existence. . . ".[97]

Almost all the descendants of the Brazilian colonists became solid members of the upper middle classes. By 1992, 50 percent of Jews in Porto Alegre had a vacation home, and a survey that same year showed that of those under forty in the Porto Alegre Jewish community 78 percent had college degrees.[98] For comparison, as of 2000 only 65 percent of Jews in the US under age fifty had college degrees.[99]

Some descendants of the colonists reached levels of success not even dreamed of in Zagradowka. The descendants of Quatro Irmãos settler Gregorio Ioschpe now own Iochpe-Maxion, the world's largest producer of steel wheels, with thirty-two factories across the globe.[100] Mauricio Sirotsky, who was born in Quatro Irmãos, founded the RBS group, which owns the major newspaper in Porto Alegre, Zero Hora, along with twenty TV stations, twenty-four radio stations, and seven other newspapers.[101] The Steinbruch family who today owns Brazil's largest steel company, CSN, with assets of over $US 22 billion as well as Brazil's largest textile firm and a major bank are descendants of immigrants who settled in the Philipson colony.[102] In Philipson the Steinbruch brothers were the keepers of the sacred scroll, the Torah. Abraham Steinbruch performed the ritual slaughter of kosher beef as well as the circumcision rites, weddings and other ceremonies.[103] And Moacyr Scliar, one of the most respected Jewish writers of his generation, who called Iolovitch's novel an inspiration to his own career in his preface to the 1987 second edition of *On a Clear April Morning*, was the son of Quatro Irmãos colonists.[104] The Iolovitch family, itself, boasts many successful lawyers and professionals who live in Europe and the United States as well as Brazil.

The Lord blessed Marcos Iolovitch, who passed away in 1984, with the years to see these successes so he knew that Verissimo had made the right call. Iolovitch's story was not the story of the disinherited. It was the story of a beautiful omen, a clear April morning.

Notes

Translator's Preface

1   IOLOVITCH, Marcos (1932). *Eu e Tu*, Porto Alegre: Livraria do Globo, p. 77.
2   MILLER, Jenny (2009). "An Exotic Way to Shake Up the Routine, From Corporate Cubicle to Casual Colonial in Porto Alegre, Brazil," *Transitions Abroad.com*, http://www.transitionsabroad.com/listings/living/articles/living-in-porto-alegre-brazil.shtml (accessed April 14, 2015).
3   VIEIRA, Nelson (1996). *Jewish Voices in Brazilian Literature*, Gainesville: University Press of Florida, p. 154.
4   FOLHA de São Paulo, "Ranking Universitario Folha 2014," http://ruf.folha.uol.com.br/2014/rankingdeuniversidades/ (accessed April 15, 2015).
5   INSTITUTO Cultural Marc Chagall, chagall.org.br.
6   SCLIAR, Moacyr (1991). *Caminhos da esperança: a presença judaica no Rio Grande do Sul /Pathways of hope : the Jewish presence in Rio Grande do Sul*, Porto Alegre: Instituto Cultural Judaico Marc Chagall.
7   GRIMES, William, (2011). "Brazilian Who Wrote of Jewish Identity," *New York Times*, March 14, 2011, p. D11.
8   IGEL, Regina (2008). "Os fios da talagarça," XI Congresso Internacional da ABRALIC Tessituras, Interações, Convergências 13 a 17 de julho de 2008, USP—São Paulo, Brasil, p. 1.
9   IGEL (2008), p. 2.
10 SCHOPENHAUER, Arthur, and Bailey Saunders, Thomas (1890). *The wisdom of life: being the first part of Arthur Schopenhauer's Aphorismen zur Lebensweisheit*, London: S. Sonnenschein, p. 35.
11 SCOTT, Sarah. "Martin Buber (1878—1965)," *The Internet Encyclopedia of Philosophy*, ISSN 2161-0002, http://www.iep.utm.edu/buber/#SH2b / (accessed Oct. 12, 2015).
12 "Martin Buber, 87, Dies in Israel; Renowned Jewish Philosopher," *New York Times*, June 14, 1965, p. 29, http://timesmachine.nytimes.com/timesmachine/1965/06/14/issue.html (accessed Oct. 10, 2015).
13 SCLIAR, Moacyr (1987). "Prefacio," *Numa Clara Manha de Abril*, Porto Alegre: Movimiento, p. 8.
14 MARTINS, Justino (1940). "Entre Duas Chicaras de Cafezinho," Porto Alegre: *Revista do Globo*, Jan. 13, 1940, p. 28.

15 LAYTANO, Dante de (1936). "Panorama de uma geracoa, coloquio com Marcos Iolovitch," *Jornal da Manha*, July 21, 1936, p. 1.

16 IOLOVITCH, Marcos (1949). *Preces Profanas*, Porto Alegre: Livraria do Globo, p. 73.

17 TORRESINI, Elizabeth W. R. (1999). *Editora Globo: Uma Aventura Editorial nos Anos 30 e 40*, Porto Alegre: Editora da Universidade Federal do Rio Grande do Sul, pp. 52-53.

18 In 1933 Germans and people of German descent made up 20 percent of Rio Grande do Sul's population.

19 See statement by Iolovitch that he studied philosophy with Jesuit professor Werner and later in law school in MARTINS (1940) and discussion of Jesuit professors of philosophy in Porto Alegre in GERTZ, Rene Ernaini (2002). *O aviador e o carroceiro: política, etnia e religião no Rio Grande do Sul dos anos 1920*, Porto Alegre: EDIPUCRS, chapters IV and VI; and GRIJÓ, Luiz Alberto (2012). "Os soldados de Deus: religião e política na Faculdade de Direito de Porto Alegre na primeira metade do século XX," *Revista Brasileira de História*, 32(64), 279-298.

20 MORAES, Carlos Dante de (1979). "Condiciones Historicos-Sociais da Literatura Rio-Grandense," *O Ensaio literário no Rio Grande do Sul: 1868-1960*, edited by F. L. Chaves, Rio de Janeiro, RJ: Livros Técnicos e Científicos Editora, p. 151.

21 ANDRADE, Mário de, and Sonia Sachs (1993). *Vida literária*, São Paulo: Hucitec u.a., p. 116.

22 MORAES (1979), p. 151.

23 MARTINS (1940) and Laytano (1936).

24 MARTINS (1940).

25 TOLSTOY, Leo, and Rosengrant, Judson (2012). *Childhood, boyhood, youth*, London: Penguin Books, p. 5.

26 CHRISTIAN, Reginald Frank. (1969). *Tolstoy: a critical introduction*, London: Cambridge U.P., p. 26.

27 LAYTANO (1936).

28 MOTA, Carlos Guilherme (1978). *Ideologia da cultura brasileira, 1933–1974: pontos de partida para uma revisão histórica*, São Paulo: Editora Ática, p. 178 (note).

29 SCLIAR, Moacyr (1998). "Uma Carta Que Vem Do Passado," *Revista ZH*, May 31, 1998, p. 3.

Chapter 1

1 Here the author is calling upon the immigrant experience in Brazil to describe the German Mennonite immigrant settlements that surrounded Zagradowka. He uses the Portuguese phrase *linhas coloniais*, a colloquial term to denote immigrant settlements used almost exclusively in southern Brazil, to refer to immigrant settlements in Ukraine.

Chapter 8

1 This paragraph was written in the late 1930s before the full extent of the Holocaust was implemented or known.

Chapter 25

1   Mil-reis were the Brazilian currency until 1942. When the author's family moved back to Porto Alegre, approximately 1927, one *real* was worth about twelve US cents.

Afterword

1   IOLOVITCH, Marcos (1987). *Numa Clara Manha de Abril,* Porto Alegre: Movimiento, p. 10.

2   SLUTSKY, Yehuda (2007). "Kherson." In Encyclopedia Judaica, Detroit: Macmillan Reference, vol. 12, pp. 144-145.

3   The lure of agricultural life might not have been the only factor in Yossef's decision to emigrate. Yossef had been blessed with male offspring and recent changes in Russia's laws covering conscription could have weighed heavily on his mind. He might have wanted to get them out of Russia before the changes were completely implemented. For it was in 1912, just a year before the Iolovitch family's emigration that the Russian Duma passed a statute declaring that "a male above the age of fifteen could not 'opt out of Russian citizenship' unless he had completed his army service . . . [which] clearly targeted Jewish emigration [as opting out of Russian citizenship was part of the emigration process]." PETROVSKY-SHTERN, Yohanan (2009). *Jews in the Russian Army, 1827-1917*, New York: Cambridge University Press, p. 245.

4   JEFFERSON, Thomas. Letter to John Jay, Aug. 23, 1785, Library of Congress, Washington, D.C. (DLC) Jefferson Quotes and Family Letters, Thomas Jefferson, Monticello.

5   *Encyclopedia Britannica.* Alexander I—Emperor of Russia, by Daria Olivier, https://www.britannica.com/biography/Alexander-I-emperor-of-Russia.

6   *Encyclopedia Britannica.* Partitions of Poland. https://www.britannica.com/event/Partitions-of-Poland.

7   DEKEL-CHEN, Jonathan (2010). "Agriculture," in *The Yivo Encyclopedia of Jews in Eastern Europe.* http://www.yivoencyclopedia.org/article.aspx/Agriculture, accessed July 20, 2014.

8   TABUACH, Shimshon (1972). "Agriculture." In *Encyclopaedia Judaica*, Jerusalem: Ketter Publishing, pp. 404-415.

9   Ibid., p. 407; and KLIER, John D. (1995). *Imperial Russia's Jewish Question, 1855-1881*, Cambridge: Cambridge University Press, pp. 301-302.

10   EPP, Jacob D. (2013). *A Mennonite in Russia: the diaries of Jacob D. Epp, 1851-1880*, Toronto: University of Toronto Press, pp. 75-130.

11   TABUACH, p. 407.

12   DEKEL-CHEN.

13   MAKUCH, Andrii (1993). "Mennonites," in *Internet Encyclopedia of Ukraine*, http://www.encyclopediaofukraine.com/display.asp?linkpath=pages%5CM%5CE%5CMennonites.htm.

14   ENS, Gerhard (1989). "Gerhard Lohrenz: His Life and Contributions," in *Mennonites in Russia 1788-1988: Essays in Honour of Gerhard Lohrenz*, Winnipeg: CMBC Publications; and LOHRENZ, Gerhard (1959). "Zagradovka Mennonite Settlement (Kherson Oblast, Ukraine)," *Global Anabaptist Mennonite Encyclopedia Online*, http://gameo.org/index.php?title=Zagradovka_Mennonite_Settlement_(Kherson_Oblast,_Ukraine)&oldid=116340.

15   IOLOVITCH, *Numa Clara Manha de Abril*, pp. 10-11.

16 DUBNOW, Semen M. (1920). "From the Accession of Nicholas II to the Present Day.", in *History of the Jews in Russia and Poland from the Earliest times to the Present Day,* vol. 3, Philadelphia: Jewish Publication Society of America, pp. 24-25.

17 ROSENTHAL, Max (1905). "Agricultural Colonies in the Argentine Republic (Argentina)," *The Jewish Encyclopedia,* http://www.jewishencyclopedia.com/articles/905-agricultural-colonies-in-the-argentine-republic-argentina.

18 HIRSCH, Maurice (1891). "My Views on Philanthropy," *North American Review* 153, no. 416 (July 1891), p. 3.

19 NORMAN, Theodore (1985). *An outstretched arm: a history of the Jewish Colonization Association,* London: Routledge & K. Paul, p. 14.

20 Ibid., p. 2.

21 HIRSCH, p. 3.

22 NORMAN, p. xii.

23 ROZENBLUM, Serge-Allain (2006). *Le Baron de Hirsch, Un financier au service de l'humanité,* Paris: Punctum Editions, p. 216.

24 HIRSCH, p. 2.

25 NORMAN, pp.19-20.

26 Ibid., p. 11.

27 Ibid., p. 19.

28 ROSENTHAL, Agricultural Colonies....

29 FRIEDMAN, Evan (2014). Personal interview with translator.

30 IOLOVITCH, *Numa Clara Manha de Abril,* p. 9.

31 For more information on the Baron Hirsch communities in Connecticut see MCDANNELL, Colleen (2004). *Picturing Faith,* New Haven: Yale University Press; and BLOCKER, Merrie (2017). "Jewish Farmers in Connecticut," *Thebaronhirschcommunity. org.*

32 LESSER, Jeff (1991). *Jewish Colonization in Rio Grande Do Sul, 1904-1925,* São Paulo: Centro de Estudos de Demografia Historica da America Latina, p. 24.

33 GRITTI, Isabel Rosa (1997). *Imigração judaica no Rio Grande do Sul: a Jewish Colonization Association e a colonização de Quatro Irmãos,* Porto Alegre: Martins Livreiro-Editor, p. 19.

34 NORMAN, p. 90.

35 COSTA, Geraldino da (2004). "Colônia Philippson," in *Anos de Amor, a Imigração Judaica no Rio Grande do Sul,* Porto Alegre: Federacão Israelita do Rio Grande do Sul, p. 1.

36 COSTA, "Colônia Philippson," p. 1; and LESSER, Jeff (1989). "Pawns of the Powerful, Jewish Immigration to Brazil 1904-1945," PhD diss., New York University, pp. 27-57.

37 OULMONT, Philippe (2012). *Pierre Denis, Français libre et citoyen du monde: entre Monnet et de Gaulle,* Paris: Nouveau Monde editions, p. 272.

38 DENIS, Pierre (1911). *Brazil,* London: T.F. Unwin, p. 296.

39 LESSER, *Jewish Colonization in Rio Grande...,* p. 47.

40 BACK, Leon (1956). "Comunidades Judaicas," in *Enciclopedia Rio-Grandense,* Canoas: Editora Regional, vol. 4, p. 324.

41 DIAS, José Roberto de Souza (1986). *Caminhos de ferro do Rio Grande do Sul,* São Paulo: Editora Rios, pp. 99-103.

42 HEUFFEL, Evelyne (2012). "Philippson: uma colônia judaica singular?," *WebMosaica* 4, p. 124, http://seer.ufrgs.br/index.php/webmosaica/article/view/37754/24362.

43 LESSER, *Jewish Colonization in Rio Grande...,* p. 29.

44 GRITTI, p. 39.

45 Ibid., p. 19.

46 LESSER, Pawns of the Powerful, p. 25.

47   ROZENBLUM, p. 254.
48   ALLEGRE, Ch. "Franz Philippson, banquier: 1871-1914", diss., ULB, History Department, 1997-1998, quoted in HEUFFEL, Evelyne (2012). "Philippson: uma colônia judaica singular?," *WebMosaica* 4, p. 124, http://seer.ufrgs.br/index.php/webmosaica/article/view/37754/24362.
49   US DEPARTMENT OF STATE. "Brazilian Immigration Regulations, 1907 Presidential Decree No. 6455 of April 19, 1907," in *Papers relating to the foreign relations of the United States / transmitted to Congress with the annual message of the President*, Washington: G.P.O., 1910, pp. 95-107.
50   GRITTI, pp. 47 and 63.
51   CUNHA, Ernesto A. Lassance (1908). *Rio Grande do Sul,* Contribução para o estudo de suas condições *economicas.* Rio de Janeiro: Imprensa Nacional, p. 11.
52   CARNEIRO, Maria Luiza Tucci (2003). Preface to *Memorias da Colonia de Quatro Irmãos,* by Marcos Feldman, São Paulo: Editora Maayanot, p. 24.
53   IOLOVITCH, *Numa Clara Manha de Abril,* pp. 19-20.
54   GRITTI, p. 43.
55   IOLOVITCH, *Numa Clara Manha de Abril,* p. 22.
56   GRITTI, p. 41.
57   Ibid., pp. 54-55.
58   LESSER, Jeffrey (1996). "Colonial Survival and Foreign Relations in Rio Grande do Sul, Brazil: The Jewish Colonization Association Colony of Quatro Irmãos, 1904-1925," in *The Jewish Diaspora in Latin America*, edited by David Shenin and Lois Barr. New York: Garland Publishing, pp. 145-148.
59   IOLOVITCH, *Numa Clara Manha de Abril,* p. 27.
60   GRITTI, p. 46.
61   Ibid., p. 47.
62   IBGE, Brazilian Institute of Geography and Statistics. "Tabela 1.6—População nos Censos Demográficos, segundo os municípios, das capitais—1872/2010," *Sinopse Censo Demográfico 2010.*
63   For further descriptions of Porto Alegre in 1916 see MARCOS, Ronaldo B. *Porto Alegre, Uma Historia Fotografica,* http://ronaldofotografia.blogspot.com; and PENSAVENTO, Sandra J. (2008). "O que se lia na velha Porto Alegre," In *Impresso no Brasil,* São Paulo: Editora UNESP, pp. 439-455; as well as photos at VAZ, Tiago (2009). A Fundação do Inter—Porto Alegre entre 1901 e 1916, http://www.supremaciacolorada.com/2008/12/ao-preo-fixo.html.
64   COSTA, Lamartine da (2005). *Atlas do esporte no Brasil,* Rio de Janeiro: Shape Editora e Promoções Ltda., p. 3-27.
65   FISHER, John R. (1997). *The economic aspects of Spanish imperialism in America, 1492-1810,* Liverpool: Liverpool University Press, p. 89.
66   SLATTA, Richard W. (1994). *The cowboy encyclopedia,* Santa Barbara, Calif.: ABC-CLIO, p. 160.
67   FEE, Fundacao de Economia e Estatisticas do Governo do Estado Rio Grande do Sul. "Exportações segundo a Nomenclatura Comum do Mercosul (2013-2015)," Table 17.
68   COSTA, Eimar Bones da, Fonseca, Ricardo, Schmitt, Ricardo (eds.) (2015). *História Ilustrada do Rio Grande do Sul,* Porto Alegre: Já Editores, p. 49.
69   CARVALHO FILHO, Irineu de, and Leonardo Monasterio, "How Bodo Became Brazilian: European Migration to Southern Brazil Before World War I", paper presented at the Third Migration and Development Conference, Paris, France, September 10-11, 2010, pp. 6-7.

70 SCHEINA, Robert L. (2003). *Latin America's Wars: The age of the Caudillo, 1791-1899*, Washington, D.C.: Brassey's, Inc., p. 153.
71 KITTLESON, Roger A. (2006). *The Practice of Politics in Postcolonial Brazil, Porto Alegre, 1845-1895*, Pittsburgh: University of Pittsburgh Press, pp. 48-73.
72 HIRSCH, p. 2.
73 CASTLEMAN, Reginald, Consul. Political report to the Embassy, Dec. 6, 1933, National Archives II, RG84/Stack350/Row 37 Porto Alegre, Brazil Consular Posts UD 691, vol. 7, class 800. College Park, Maryland: US National Archives, p. 2.
74 ADAM, Thomas (2005). *Germany and the Americas: culture, politics, and history*, Santa Barbara, California: ABC-CLIO, p. 337.
75 IBGE, Brazilian Institute of Geography and Statistics. "Tabela 2094—População residente por cor ou raça e religião," *Censo Demografico, 2010*.
76 MORGAN, Edward, Ambassador. "Letter to the Secretary of State on General Conditions of Brazil, Aug. 25, 1920," National Archives II NAM519 (Internal Affairs of Brazil), roll 4, 832/196. College Park, Maryland: US National Archives, p. 3.
77 FARRAND, E. Kitchel, Vice-Consul. "Monthly report on Political Conditions for September, 1925 in the Porto Alegre Consular District, Oct. 3, 1925," National Archives II NAM519 (Internal Affairs of Brazil), roll 6, 832/540. College Park, Maryland: US National Archives, p. 3.
78 VERÍSSIMO, Erico (1954). *Lembrança de Pôrto Alegre*, Rio de Janeiro: Editôra Globo.
79 JACOBSEN, Alfred S. "State of Rio Grande do Sul, Report to U.S. Consul C. R. Nasmith," April 29, 1931, National Archives II, RG84/Stack350/Row 37 Porto Alegre, Brazil Consular Posts UD 691, vol 84/850, College Park, Maryland: US National Archives, p. 4.
80 Ibid.
81 BRADLEY, John R., Consul. "Some Comments on the Nationality, Number and Kinds of Business Houses in the State of Rio Grande do Sul," November 27, 1923, National Archives II, RG84/Stack350/Row 37 Porto Alegre, Brazil Consular Posts UD 691, vol 6, College Park, Maryland: US National Archives, p. 8.
82 LESSER, Jeffrey (1995). *Welcoming the Undesirables, Brazil and the Jewish Question*, California: University of California Press, p. 18.
83 LEE, Samuel, Consul. "Political Conditions in the State of Rio Grande do Sul, April 28, 1917," National Archives II NAM 519, roll 4 832/142. College Park, Maryland: US National Archives, p. 1.
84 GUTFREIND, Ieda (2010). "Imigração judaica no Rio Grande do Sul Pogroms na terra gaúcha?," *WebMosaica*, 2, pp. 86-88, http://www.seer.ufrgs.br/index.php/webmosaica/article/view/15547.
85 HUBLEIN, Fred E., American Vice-Consul. POA, "Letter to Ambassador Edwin Morgan, Dec. 6, 1926," National Archives II, RG84/Stack350/Row 37 Porto Alegre, Brazil Consular Posts UD 691, vol. 53/800, p. 2. For further discussion of economic difficulties caused by the violence and political unrest see

US DEPARTMENT OF STATE. "Monthly Reports on Political Condition in the Porto Alegre Consular District" (microfiche), National Archives II NAM 519 roll 5 832/302, Sept. 4, 1923, p. 2, 832/305, Nov. 2, 1923, p. 2, 832/333, April 1, 1924, p. 2-3; roll 6 832/432, Sept. 1, 1924, p. 2, 832/478, Dec 1, 1924, p. 3, 832/487, Jan. 3, 1925, p. 2-3, 832/495, Feb. 2, 1925, p. 2, 832/509, p. 2, 832/540, Oct. 3, 1925, p. 3, roll 7 832/592, Sept. 3, 1926, p. 1, 832/617, Jan 31, 1927, p. 4, 832/628, May 7, 1927, College Park, Maryland: US National Archives; and

US DEPARTMENT OF STATE. "Monthly reports on the Porto Alegre Consular Districts" (documents), National Archives II, RG84/Stack350/Row 37 Porto Alegre, Brazil Consular Posts UD 691, vol. 7, Aug. 1, 1924, pp. 2-3, vol. 52, Feb. 5, 1926, p. 1. College Park, Maryland: US National Archives.

86 US DEPARTMENT OF STATE. "Report on Rebellion of Federal Troops and Revolutionary Activities in the State of Rio Grande do Sul," National Archives II NAM 519 roll 7 832/607, Nov. 20, 1926. College Park, Maryland: US National Archives, p. 2.

87 IOLOVITCH, *Numa Clara Manha de Abril*, p. 45.

88 For an in-depth discussion of these Jewish peddlers see GILL, Lorena Almeida (2001). *Clienteltchiks: os Judeus de prestação em Pelotas (RS), 1920-1945*, Pelotas: Editora e Gráfica Universitária.

89 PESAVENTO, Sandra J. (2002). *O imaginario da cidade. Visoes literarias do Urbano*, Porto Alegre: Editora da Universidade Federal Rio Grando do Sul, p. 291.

90 LOVE, Joseph L. (1971). *Rio Grande do Sul and Brazilian Regionalism*, Stanford: Stanford University Press, p. 130.

91 PORTO ALEGRE FERIA do LIVRO. Executive Commission email to translator of Aug. 25, 2014.

92 IOLOVITCH, *Numa Clara Manha de Abril*, p. 99.

93 LEE, p. 1.

94 FISCHER, Luis Augusto (2008). "A era Erico e depois," in *História geral do Rio Grande do Sul*, co-ordinated by Nelson Boeira and Tau Golin, vol. 4, 427-435, Passo Fundo, RS: Méritos Editora, p. 437.

95 CANDIDA-SMITH, Richard (2013). "Érico Veríssimo, a Brazilian Cultural Ambassador in the United States," *Revista Tempo* 17, nr. 3, p. 170.

96 For further background on Livraria, Revista, and Editora Globo see BARCELLOS, Marília de Araujo (2002) "O editor Érico Veríssimo e a produção editorial da Globo," Paper presented in NP04—The nucleus on research on publishing (Núcleo de Pesquisa Produção Editorial), XXV Annual Congress on the Science of Communcation (Congresso Anual em Ciência da Comunicação), Salvador de Bahia, Brazil, September 4-5, 2002; and TORRESINI, Elizabeth W. R. (1999). *Editora Globo: Uma Aventura Editorial nos Anos 30 e 40*, São Paulo: Editora da Universidade de São Paulo; and PUCRS. (Pontificia Universidade Catolica do RGS). "Revista do Globo," http://www.pucrs.br/delfos/?p=globo.

97 HIRSCH, p. 2.

98 BRUMER, Anita (1994). *Identidade em mudança: pesquisa sociológica sobre os judeus no Rio Grande do Sul*, Porto Alegre, RS: Federação Israelita do Rio Grande do Sul, p. 83.

99 MAZUR, Allan (2007). *A Statistical Portrait of American Jews into the 21st Century*, Syracuse: Garret, 2007, p. 8.

100 IOCHPE-MAXION. http://www.iochpe.com.br.

101 NAIDITCH, Suzana. "A história da RBS," *Exame.com*, May 13, 2011; and GRUPORBS, http://www.gruporbs.com.br.

102 CSN, Companhia Siderurgica Nacional. www.csn.com.br, accessed July 7, 2014.

103 BACK, p. 323; and SCLIAR (1991), p. 4.

104 SCLIAR, Moacyr (1987). preface to *Numa Clara Manha de Abril*, by Marcos Iolovitch, Porto Alegre: Editora Movimiento, pp. 7-8.

References

ADAM, Thomas. *Germany and the Americas: culture, politics, and history.* Santa Barbara, California: ABC-CLIO, 2005.

ALLEGRE, C. *Franz Philippson, banquier: 1871–1914.* ULB, History Department, 1997–1998. Diss., quoted in HEUFFEL, Evelyne. "Philippson: uma colônia judaica singular?" *WebMosaica* 4 (2012): 124. Accessed October 4, 2014. http://seer.ufrgs.br/index.php/webmosaica/article/view/37754/24362.

BACK, Leon. "Comunidades Judaicas." In *Enciclopedia Rio-Grandense*, edited by Klaus Becker, vol. 4, pp. 323-333. Canoas: Editora Regional, 1956.

BARCELLOS, Marília de Araujo. "O editor Érico Veríssimo e a produção editorial da Globo." Paper presented in NP04—The nucleus on research on publishing (Núcleo de Pesquisa Produção Editorial), XXV Annual Congress on the Science of Communication (Congresso Anual em Ciência da Comunicação), Salvador de Bahia, Brazil, September 2002. https://www.academia.edu/1382589/O_EDITOR_ÉRICO_VERÍSSIMO_EA_PRODUÇÃO_EDITORIAL_DA_GLOBO. Accessed April 21, 2015.

BIDELEUX, Robert, and Jeffries, Ian. *A History of Eastern Europe: Crisis and Change.* London: Routledge, 1998.

BLOCKER, Merrie. "Jewish Farmers in Connecticut." *Thebaronhirschcommunity.org*, posted April 4, 2017. https://thebaronhirschcommunity.org/category/usa/connecticut/. Accessed September 12, 2019.

BRADLEY, John R., Consul. "Some Comments on the Nationality, Number and Kinds of Business Houses in the State of Rio Grande do Sul," November 27, 1923. National Archives II, RG84/Stack350/Row 37 Porto Alegre, Brazil Consular Posts UD 691, vol. 6, p. 8. College Park, Maryland: US National Archives.

BRUMER, Anita. *Identidade em mudança: pesquisa sociológica sobre os judeus no Rio Grande do Sul.* Porto Alegre, RS: Federação Israelita do Rio Grande do Sul, 1994.

CANDIDA-SMITH, Richard. "Érico Veríssimo, a Brazilian Cultural Ambassador in the United States." *Revista Tempo* 17, no. 3 (2013): 147–173. http://history.berkeley.edu/sites/default/files/%C3%89rico%20Ver%C3%ADssimo%20A%20Brazilian%20Cultural%20Ambassador.pdf. Accessed August 10, 2014.

CARNEIRO, Maria Luiza Tucci. Preface to *Memorias da Colonia de Quatro Irmãos,* by Marcos Feldman, 19–26. São Paulo: Editora Maayanot, 2003.

CARVALHO FILHO, Irineu de, and Leonardo Monasterio. "How Bodo Became Brazilian: European Migration to Southern Brazil Before World War I". Paper presented at the Third Migration and Development Conference, Paris, France, September 2010. http://www.parisschoolofeconomics.eu/IMG/pdf/de_Carvalho_Filho_Monasterio_How_Bodo_Became_Brazilian__European_Migration_to_Southern_Brazil_Before_World_War.pdf. Accessed April 6, 2015.

CASTLEMAN, Reginald, Consul. Political report to the Embassy, Dec. 6, 1933. National Archives II, RG84/Stack350/Row 37 Porto Alegre, Brazil Consular Posts UD 691, vol. 7, class 800, p. 2. College Park, Maryland: US National Archives.

COSTA, Eimar Bones da, Fonseca, Ricardo, Schmitt, Ricardo, eds. *História Ilustrada do Rio Grande do Sul.* Porto Alegre: Já Editores, 2015.

COSTA, Geraldino da. "Colônia Philippson." In *Anos de Amor, a Imigração Judaica no Rio Grande do Sul,* edited by Jacques Wainberg, 69–99. Porto Alegre: Federacão Israelita do Rio Grande do Sul, 2004.

COSTA, Lamartine da. *Atlas do esporte no Brasil.* Rio de Janeiro: Shape Editora e Promoções Ltda, 2005.

CSN, Companhia Siderurgica Nacional. www.csn.com.br. Accessed July 7, 2014.

CUNHA, Ernesto A. Lassance. *Rio Grande do Sul, Contribucao para o estudo de suas condicoes economicas.* Rio de Janiero: Imprensa Nacional, 1908.

DEKEL-CHEN, Jonathan. "Agriculture." *The Yivo Encyclopedia of Jews in Eastern Europe.* 2010. http://www.yivoencyclopedia.org/article.aspx/Agriculturehttp://www.yivoencyclopedia.org/article.aspx/Agriculture. Accessed July 20, 2014.

DENIS, Pierre. *Brazil.* Translated by Bernard Miall. London: T.F. Unwin, 1911. https://archive.org/details/brazilde00deniuoft. Accessed April 26, 2017.

DIAS, José Roberto de Souza. *Caminhos de ferro do Rio Grande do Sul.* São Paulo: Editora Rios, 1986.

DUBNOW, Semen M. "From the Accession of Nicholas II to the Present Day." In *History of the Jews in Russia and Poland from the Earliest times to the Present Day,* vol. 3. Translated by Israel Friedlaender. Philadelphia: Jewish Publication Society of America, 1920.

ENCYCLOPAEDIA BRITANNICA. "Partitions of Poland." https://www.britannica.com/event/Partitions-of-Poland. Accessed June 17, 2017.

———. "Alexander I—Emperor of Russia," by Daria Olivier. https://www.britannica.com/biography/Alexander-I-emperor-of-Russia. Accessed June 18, 2017.

ENS, Gerhard. "Gerhard Lohrenz: His Life and Contributions." In *Mennonites in Russia 1788-1988: Essays in Honour of Gerhard Lohrenz,* edited by John Friesen, 1–10. Winnipeg: CMBC Publications, 1989.

EPP, Jacob D. *A Mennonite in Russia: the diaries of Jacob D. Epp, 1851–1880.* Translated by Harvey L. Dyck. Toronto: University of Toronto Press, 2013.

FARRAND, E. Kitchel, Vice-Consul. "Monthly report on Political Conditions for September, 1925 in the Porto Alegre Consular District, Oct. 3, 1925." National Archives II NAM519 (Internal Affairs of Brazil), roll 6, 832/540, p. 3. College Park, Maryland: US National Archives.

FEE, Fundacao de Economia e Estatisticas do Governo do Estado Rio Grande do Sul. "Exportações segundo a Nomenclatura Comum do Mercosul (2013–2015)": Table 17. http://www.fee.rs.gov.br/indicadores/indice-das-exportacoes/serie-historica/. Accessed April 26, 2017.

FISCHER, Luis Augusto. "A era Erico e depois." In *História geral do Rio Grande do Sul*, co-ordinated by Nelson Boeira and Tau Golin, vol. 4, 427–435. Passo Fundo, RS: Méritos Editora, 2008.

FISHER, John R. *The economic aspects of Spanish imperialism in America, 1492–1810*. Liverpool: Liverpool University Press, 1997.

FOLHA de São Paulo. "Ranking Universitario Folha 2016." http://ruf.folha.uol.com.br/2016/ranking-de-universidades. Accessed May 1, 2017.

FRIEDMAN, Evan. Personal interview with translator, March 2014.

GERTZ, Rene Ernaini. *O aviador e o carroceiro: política, etnia e religião no Rio Grande do Sul dos anos 1920*, Porto Alegre: EDIPUCRS, 2002.

GILL, Lorena Almeida. *Clienteltchiks: os Judeus de prestação em Pelotas (RS), 1920–1945*. Pelotas: Editora e Gráfica Universitária, 2001.

GRIJO, Luiz Alberto. "Os soldados de Deus: religião e política na Faculdade de Direito de Porto Alegre na primeira metade do século XX." *Revista Brasileira de História* 32, no. 64 (2012): 279-298.

GRIMES, William. "Brazilian Who Wrote of Jewish Identity." *New York Times*, March 14, 2011.

GRITTI, Isabel Rosa. *Imigração judaica no Rio Grande do Sul: a Jewish Colonization Association e a colonização de Quatro Irmãos*. Porto Alegre: Martins Livreiro-Editor, 1997.

GRUPO RBS. http://www.gruporbs.com.br. Accessed July 2, 2014.

GUTFREIND, Ieda. "Imigração judaica no Rio Grande do Sul Pogroms na terra gaúcha?" *WebMosaica* 2 (2010): 84–91. http://www.seer.ufrgs.br/index.php/webmosaica/article/view/15547. Accessed Oct. 4, 2014.

HIRSCH, Maurice. "My Views on Philanthropy." *North American Review* 153, no. 416 (July 1891): 1–4. http://www.jstor.org/stable/25102205. Accessed Nov. 20, 2014.

HUBLEIN, Fred E, American Vice-Consul. POA, "Letter to Ambassador Edwin Morgan, Dec. 6, 1926." National Archives II, RG84/Stack350/Row 37 Porto Alegre, Brazil Consular Posts UD 691, vol. 53/800, p. 2. College Park, Maryland, US National Archives.

HEUFFEL, Evelyne. "Philippson: uma colônia judaica singular?" *WebMosaica* 4 (2012): 121–147. http://seer.ufrgs.br/index.php/webmosaica/article/view/37754/24362. Accessed Oct. 4, 2014 .

IBGE, Brazilian Institute of Geography and Statistics. "Tabela 2094—População residente por cor ou raça e religião." *Censo Demografico, 2010*. http://www.sidra.ibge.gov.br/bda/tabela/listabl.asp?z=cd&o=7&i=P&c=2094. Accessed April 26, 2017.

_____. "Tabela 1.6 - População nos Censos Demográficos, segundo os municípios, das capitais—1872/2010." *Sinopse Censo Demográfico 2010.* http://www.censo2010.ibge.gov. br/sinopse/index.php?dados=6&uf=00. Accessed April 10, 2015.

IGEL, Regina (2008). "Os fios da talagarça." XI Congresso Internacional da ABRALIC Tessituras, Interações, Convergências, 13 a 17 de julho de 2008, USP—São Paulo, Brasil.

IOCHPE-MAXION. http://www.iochpe.com.br. Accessed June 5, 2014.

IOLOVITCH, Marcos. *Eu e Tu.* Porto Alegre: Livraria do Globo, 1932.

_____. *Numa Clara Manha de Abril.* Porto Alegre: Livraria do Globo, 1940.

_____. *Numa Clara Manha de Abril.* Porto Alegre: Editora Movimento, 1987.

_____. *Preces Profanas.* Porto Alegre: Livraria do Globo, 1949.

JACOBSEN, Alfred S. "State of Rio Grande do Sul, Report to U.S. Consul C. R. Nasmith, April 29, 1931". National Archives II, RG84/Stack350/Row 37 Porto Alegre, Brazil Consular Posts UD 691, vol. 84/850, p. 4. College Park, Maryland: US National Archives.

JEFFERSON, Thomas. Letter to John Jay, Aug. 23, 1785. Library of Congress, Washington, D.C. (DLC) Jefferson Quotes and Family Letters, Thomas Jefferson, Monticello. http:// tjrs.monticello.org/letter/69#X3184736. Accessed May 7, 2015.

KITTLESON, Roger A. *The Practice of Politics in Postcolonial Brazil, Porto Alegre, 1845–1895.* Pittsburgh: University of Pittsburgh Press, 2006.

KLIER, John D. *Imperial Russia's Jewish Question, 1855–1881.* Cambridge: Cambridge University Press, 1995.

JEWISH VIRTUAL LIBRARY. "Porto Alegre." http://www.jewishvirtuallibrary.org/jsource/ judaica/ejud_0002_0016_0_16006.html. Accessed May 1, 2015.

LAYTANO, Dante de. "Panorama de uma geracoa, coloquio com Marcos Iolovitch." *Jornal da Manha*, July 21, 1936

LEE, Samuel, Consul. "Political Conditions in the State of Rio Grande do Sul, April 28, 1917." National Archives II NAM 519, roll 4 832/142, p. 1. College Park, Maryland: US National Archives.

LESSER, Jeff. "Pawns of the Powerful, Jewish Immigration to Brazil 1904–1945." PhD diss., New York University, 1989.

_____. *Jewish Colonization in Rio Grande Do Sul, 1904–1925.* São Paulo: Centro de Estudos de Demografia Historica da America Latina, Universidade de São Paulo, Faculdade de Filosofia, Letras e Ciencias Humanas, 1991.

LESSER, Jeffrey. *Welcoming the Undesirables, Brazil and the Jewish Question.* California: University of California Press, 1995.

_____. "Colonial Survival and Foreign Relations in Rio Grande do Sul, Brazil: The Jewish Colonization Association Colony of Quatro Irmãos, 1904–1925." In *The Jewish Diaspora in Latin America*, edited by David Shenin and Lois Barr, 143–160. New York: Garland Publishing, 1996.

LOHRENZ, Gerhard. "Zagradovka Mennonite Settlement (Kherson Oblast, Ukraine)," originally published 1959. *Global Anabaptist Mennonite Encyclopedia Online.* http://

gameo.org/index.php?title=Zagradovka_Mennonite_Settlement_(Kherson_Oblast, _ Ukraine)&oldid=116340. Accessed November 26, 2014.

LOVE, Joseph L. *Rio Grande do Sul and Brazilian Regionalism*. Stanford: Stanford University Press, 1971.

MAKUCH, Andrii. "Mennonites," originally published 1993. *Internet Encyclopedia of Ukraine*. http://www.encyclopediaofukraine.com/display.asp?linkpath=pages%5CM%5CE%5CMennonites.htm. Accessed May 1, 2017.

MARCOS, Ronaldo B. *Porto Alegre, Uma Historia Fotografica*. http://ronaldofotografia. blogspot.com. Accessed February 26, 2015.

MARTINS, Justino. "Entre Duas Chicaras de Cafezinho." *Revista do Globo*, Jan. 13, 1940.

MAZUR, Allan. *A Statistical Portrait of American Jews into the 21st Century*. Syracuse: Garret, 2007. http://faculty.maxwell.syr.edu/amazur/Jews.pdf. Accessed May 1, 2017.

MCDANNELL, Colleen. *Picturing Faith*. New Haven: Yale University Press, 2004.

MILLER, Jenny. "An Exotic Way to Shake Up the Routine, From Corporate Cubicle to Casual Colonial in Porto Alegre, Brazil." *Transitions Abroad.com*, published 2009. http://www.transitionsabroad.com/listings/living/articles/living-in-porto-alegre-brazil.shtml. Accessed April 14, 2015.

MORAES, Carlos Dante de. "Condiciones Historicos-Sociais da Literatura Rio-Grandense." In *O Ensaio literário no Rio Grande do Sul: 1868-1960*, edited by F. L. Chaves. Rio de Janeiro, RJ: Livros Técnicos e Científicos Editora, 1979.

MORGAN, Ambassador Edward. "Letter to the Secretary of State on General Conditions of Brazil, Aug. 25, 1920." National Archives II NAM519 (Internal Affairs of Brazil), roll 4 832/196, p. 3. College Park, Maryland: US National Archives.

MOTA, Carlos Guilherme. *Ideologia da cultura brasileira, 1933–1974: pontos de partida para uma revisão histórica*. São Paulo: Editora Ática, 1978.

NAIDITCH, Suzana. "A história da RBS." *Exame.com*, May 13, 2011. http://exame.abril. com.br/negocios/noticias/a-historia-da-rbs-m0039798. Accessed May 1, 2017.

NORMAN, Theodore. *An outstretched arm: a history of the Jewish Colonization Association*. London: Routledge & K. Paul, 1985.

OULMONT, Philippe. *Pierre Denis, Français libre et citoyen du monde: entre Monnet et de Gaulle*. Paris: Nouveau Monde editions, 2012.

PESAVENTO, Sandra J. *O imaginario da cidade. Visoes literarias do Urbano*. Porto Alegre: Editora da Universidade Federal Rio Grando do Sul, 2002.

PESAVENTO, Sandra J. "O que se lia na velha Porto Alegre." In *Impresso no Brasil*, edited by Anibal Braganca and Marcia Abreu, 439–455. São Paulo: Editora UNESP, 2008.

PETROVSKY-SHTERN, Yohanan. *Jews in the Russian Army, 1827–1917*. New York: Cambridge University Press, 2009.

PORTO ALEGRE FERIA do LIVRO. Executive Commission email to translator dated August 25, 2014.

PUCRS (Pontificia Universidade Catolica do RGS). "Revista do Globo." http://www.pucrs. br/delfos/?p=globo. Accessed April 10, 2015.

ROSENTHAL, Herman. "May Laws." *Jewish Encyclopedia*, 1906. http://www.jewishencyclopedia.com/articles/10508-may-laws. Accessed March 31, 2017.

ROSENTHAL, Max. "Agricultural Colonies in the Argentine Republic (Argentina)." *Jewish Encyclopedia*, 1906. http://www.jewishencyclopedia.com/articles/905-agricultural-colonies-in-the-argentine-republic-argentina. Accessed April 27, 2017.

ROZENBLUM, Serge-Allain. *Le Baron de Hirsch, Un financier au service de l'humanité.* Paris: Punctum Editions, 2006.

SCHEINA, Robert L. *Latin America's Wars: The age of the Caudillo, 1791–1899.* Washington D.C.: Brassey's, Inc., 2003.

SCLIAR, Moacyr. Preface to *Numa Clara Manha de Abril,* by Marcos Iolovitch. Porto Alegre: Editora Movimiento, 1987.

SCLIAR, Moacyr. *Caminhos da Esperanca/Pathways of Hope, The Jewish presence in Rio Grande do Sul.* Porto Alegre: Instituto Cultural Judaico Marc Chagall, 1991.

SCLIAR, Moacyr. "Uma Carta Que Vem Do Passado." *Revista ZH*, May 31, 1998, p. 3.

SCOTT, Sarah. "Martin Buber (1878—1965)." *The Internet Encyclopedia of Philosophy*, ISSN 2161-0002. http://www.iep.utm.edu/buber/#SH2b/. Accessed Oct. 12, 2015.

SLATTA, Richard W. *The cowboy encyclopedia.* Santa Barbara, Calif.: ABC-CLIO, 1994.

SLUTSKY, Yehuda. "Kherson." In *Encyclopedia Judaica*, edited by Michael Berenbaum and Fred Skolnik, vol. 12, 114–115. Detroit: Macmillan Reference USA, 2007. http://go.galegroup.com/ps/i.do?id=GALE%7CCX2587511090&v=2.1&u=imcpl1111&it=r&p=GVRL&sw=w&asid=ca1fc49aa46f611d0f61f0dd0b95ce75. Accessed May 3, 2017.

TABUACH, Shimshon. "Agriculture." In *Encyclopaedia Judaica*, edited by Cecil Roth, 404–415. Jerusalem: Ketter Publishing, 1972.

TOLSTOY, Leo, and ROSENGRANT, Judson. *Childhood, boyhood, youth*, London: Penguin Books, 2012.

TORRESINI, Elizabeth W. R. *Editora Globo: Uma Aventura Editorial nos Anos 30 e 40.* São Paulo: Editora da Universidade de São Paulo, 1999.

US DEPARTMENT OF STATE. "Brazilian Immigration Regulations, 1907 Presidential Decree No. 6455 of April 19, 1907." In *Papers relating to the foreign relations of the United States / transmitted to Congress with the annual message of the President.* Washington: G.P.O., 1910.

US DEPARTMENT OF STATE. "Report on Rebellion of Federal Troops and Revolutionary Activities in the State of Rio Grande do Sul." National Archives II NAM 519 roll 7 832/607, Nov. 20, 1926, p. 2. College Park, Maryland: US National Archives.

US DEPARTMENT OF STATE a. "Monthly Reports on Political Condition in the Porto Alegre Consular District" (microfiche). National Archives II NAM 519 roll 5 832.302, Sept. 4, 1923, p. 2, 832/305, Nov. 2, 1923, p. 2, 832/333, April 1, 1924, p. 2–3; roll 6 832/432, Sept. 1, 1924, p. 2, 832/478, Dec 1, 1924, p. 3, 832/487, Jan 3. 1925, p. 2–3, 832/495, Feb. 2, 1925, p. 2, 832/509, p. 2, 832/540, Oct. 3, 1925, p. 3, roll 7 832/592, Sept. 3, 1926, p. 1, 832/617, Jan 31, 1927, p. 4, 832/628, May 7, 1927.

US DEPARTMENT OF STATE b. "Monthly reports on the Porto Alegre Consular Districts," (documents). National Archives II, RG84/Stack350/Row 37 Porto Alegre, Brazil Consular Posts UD 691, vol. 7, August 1, 1924, pp. 2–3, vol. 52, February 5, 1926, p. 1. College Park, Maryland: US National Archives.

VAZ, Tiago. "A Fundação do Inter—Porto Alegre entre 1901 e 1916," 2009. http://www.supremaciacolorada.com/2008/12/ao-preo-fixo.html. Accessed February 15, 2015.

VERÍSSIMO, Erico. *Lembrança de Pôrto Alegre*. Rio de Janeiro: Editôra Globo, 1954.

VIEIRA, Nelson. *Jewish Voices in Brazilian Literature*. Gainesville: University Press of Florida, 1996.

Index